Kristy and the Walking Disaster

**Look for these and other books
in the Baby-sitters Club series:**

Kristy and the Walking Disaster
Ann M. Martin

AN
APPLE
PAPERBACK

SCHOLASTIC INC.
New York Toronto London Auckland Sydney

ISBN 0-590-42004-6

12 11 10 9 8 7 6 5 4 3 2 1   9/8 0 1 2 3 4/9

Printed in the U.S.A.   28

First Scholastic printing, January 1989

*This book is for
the members of
the Lunch Club*

CHAPTER 1

"We're here! We're here!"

The front door to my house burst open and in barged Karen and Andrew. Karen and Andrew are my stepsister and stepbrother. Karen is six and Andrew is four, and Karen was the one doing the yelling. Andrew is sort of quiet and shy. In fact, he's very quiet and shy. He's the opposite of Karen. It's hard to believe they're brother and sister.

"Hi, you guys!" I called. I was on the upstairs landing, looking down. I ran to greet them. "I'm so glad you're here early. I'm glad your mom had to go out."

"Me too!" exclaimed Karen. She slung her knapsack on the floor.

Andrew put his down more gently. "Me too," he whispered.

I hugged Andrew and Karen, and then Karen ran off to check on things — her room, Shannon (our puppy), and Boo-Boo (our cat).

1

Andrew glanced at me and said, "Maybe David Michael wants to play catch." He looked terribly hopeful.

"He might," I said. "He's out in the back-yard. Why don't you go see."

Are you confused yet? I'll stop here so I can introduce myself and explain who all these people are. My name is Kristy Thomas. I'm thirteen and in the eighth grade. One of the most important things to know about me is that I am the president, founder, and creator of a business called the Baby-sitters Club.

David Michael is my brother. He's seven. I have two other brothers. They're in high school. Sam is fifteen and Charlie is seventeen. Up until not long ago my three brothers and I lived with our mother in a small house across town here in Stoneybrook, Connecticut. (Our parents are divorced.) Then my mom met this guy, Watson Brewer, a divorced millionaire. Practically before we knew it, she had married him and he had moved us into his house — which is a mansion.

Karen and Andrew are Watson's children. They live with us every other weekend and for two weeks during the summer. The rest of the time they live with their mother and step-father.

To be honest, I didn't like Watson much at

first. Oh, all right. I hated him. I didn't want anything to do with him, even though he likes baseball as much as I do. I even refused to meet his kids. You know what brought us together? The Baby-sitters Club. Once, in an emergency, I got a job sitting for Karen and Andrew. By the time the job was over, I thought they were the greatest kids in the world. Now I am so, so glad they're my steps.

It was a Friday afternoon, almost five o'clock. Mom and Watson were both at work. Sam was around somewhere. He was probably doing his homework. He likes to get it out of the way on Fridays so he can turn into a couch potato for the rest of the weekend. Charlie was out, but I was waiting for him to come home. Three times a week he drives me to and from meetings of the Baby-sitters Club, which are held from five-thirty until six o'clock in my old neighborhood on the other side of Stoney-brook.

I decided I better go check on the little kids. I never know *what* Karen might be up to. She's not naughty, but she's fearless and has a wild imagination. (Watson calls it "fertile," I guess meaning that any idea could grow there.)

Trying to keep track of all the people (not to mention animals) in my house is not easy, especially when Karen and Andrew are over.

Can you believe that my mom has been talking about wanting *another* kid? I can't. I love children, but there's plenty of confusion at our house as it is. Besides, my mother is at least thirty-seven.

I found Karen, Andrew, and David Michael in the backyard. They were trying to play three-man softball.

"This is so dumb!" David Michael was saying. (He was only saying that because he had just missed the ball.)

"David Michael," I said, "watch the *ball* when it's being pitched. Don't look at your *bat*. I know you want to connect the two of them, but believe me, you won't hit the ball if you don't look at it."

Karen pitched the ball again and David Michael watched it like a hawk. He swung. *Crack!* The ball sailed across the yard.

"All right! Home run!" I yelled.

I just love sports.

"Boy, thanks, Kristy!" exclaimed my brother. "That was a good tip. . . . I sure wish I could play softball or baseball on a real team, with a coach and everything."

"Me too," said Karen and Andrew.

"Hey, Kristy!" someone yelled.

"Coming!" I shouted back. It was Charlie.

He was home and ready to drive me to my club meeting.

"I gotta go, you guys. Behave yourselves, okay? Sam's home and Mom and Watson will be here soon. We'll talk about softball later."

I ran to our front drive and jumped into the car, next to Charlie.

"Ready to go visit your little friends?" he teased me.

I scowled. They are not *little* friends, and Charlie knows it. They are Claudia Kishi, Mary Anne Spier, Dawn Schafer, Mallory Pike, and Jessi Ramsey, and they are all different and special. And none of them is little. Claudia, Mary Anne, and Dawn are thirteen, like me. Jessi and Mal are eleven and in the sixth grade.

I used to live next door to Mary Anne (she's my best friend) and across the street from Claudia. Us thirteen-year-olds are eighth-graders in Stoneybrook Middle School. (Most of the kids in my new neighborhood go to private school, but Mom let my brothers and me stay in our regular public schools.)

Mary Anne Spier is the most sensitive person I know. Sometimes she's too sensitive. She'll cry over the slightest thing. And she's shy and quiet, like Andrew. But once she's your friend, you've got a friend for life. She is very loyal.

Maybe that's part of the reason Mary Anne was the first one of us to have a steady boyfriend. His name is Logan Bruno. Mary Anne lives with her dad and her kitten, Tigger. Her mom died a long time ago, so long ago that Mary Anne doesn't even remember her.

Even though I have a big mouth and I'm far from shy, Mary Anne and I are alike in some ways. For one thing, we look alike. We both have brown eyes and brown hair and are short. I'm the shortest kid in our grade, believe it or not, but Mary Anne has grown slightly. For another thing, we don't care much about clothes. Truthfully, I don't care a *thing* about clothes. My friends tease me because I always wear a turtleneck, jeans, a sweater, and sneakers. (Well, not in the summer, of course.) And Mary Anne used to have to wear this babyish stuff that her father picked out for her, but now he's not so strict and lets Mary Anne choose her own clothes, so Mary Anne is more interested in what she wears.

Boy, are Mary Anne and I different from Claudia Kishi! Claud is super-sophisticated — and totally great-looking. She's Japanese-American and gorgeous, with long, long silky, jet-black hair; dark, almond-shaped eyes; and a complexion that's to die for. She's funny and talented — you should see her artwork — and she practically has boys drooling over her, but she doesn't have a steady boyfriend like Mary Anne does. One thing about Claudia that's a problem is that she's a terrible student. To make this worse, her older sister Janine is a true genius. Janine is in high school, but she already takes college courses.

Claudia and Janine live with their parents and their grandmother Mimi. Claudia's special likes are: junk food, mysteries (especially Nancy Drew mysteries), and, of course, her art. Her artistic flair runs over into her clothes. You should see how she dresses — wild! Baggy jeans, skintight pants, miniskirts, odd layers of things, bright colors, and weird jewelry. Also, she fixes her hair differently every day, and she does things like paint her toenails with sparkles. Once, she went to school with glitter in her hair.

Dawn Schafer, who is Mary Anne's other best friend, is originally from California. She and her mom and younger brother Jeff moved here when us club members were halfway through seventh grade. They moved because her folks got divorced, and Mrs. Schafer had grown up here in Stoneybrook. A sad thing is that Jeff was so unhappy that not long ago he moved back to California to live with his father. Now Dawn's family is divided in half — and separated by a continent. In a way, this is like my own family, since my dad took off for California years ago and I never see him, but I feel luckier than Dawn. I have a new family now.

Dawn is really great, even though sometimes I'm a little jealous of her since she's so close to Mary Anne. But Dawn is independent. She "does her own thing" and couldn't care less what anyone else thinks. She's super-organized, a health-food nut, and has her own style of dress. I think of it as "California casual." Also, Dawn has the palest blue eyes and the longest, blondest hair I've ever seen.

Now — about our two younger members, Mallory Pike and Jessi Ramsey. They joined the club awhile ago after one of our original members, Stacey McGill, had to move away. (I'll tell you more about Stacey later, I promise.) Mal joined first. She's the oldest of the eight Pike kids. Our club sits for the Pikes a lot. Mallory had always been a big help to us sitters, so now that she's eleven, she's allowed to sit in the afternoons and on weekends. She's great with kids! She's patient and practical. She thinks her parents treat her like a baby, though. She desperately wants contacts instead of glasses, but she's getting braces instead. She wishes her hair were straighter. She wishes a lot of things. Mal loves reading, writing (poetry and stories), drawing, and horses.

Jessi (Jessica) Ramsey is Mal's friend. Her family moved to Stoneybrook pretty recently, and both Jessi and Mal were in the market for a best friend. When they found each other — *POW!* They have so much in common. They have the same interests (plus Jessi is a talented ballet dancer), they both think their parents treat them like babies, and they both come from really great families, although Jessi's is much smaller than Mal's. Apart from Jessi and her parents, there are just her eight-year-old sister Becca (short for Rebecca) and her baby brother Squirt, whose real name is John Philip Ramsey, Jr. Here's the one big difference between Mal and Jessi. Mal is white and Jessi is black. That hasn't mattered to either of them, but being black in Stoneybrook can be difficult. Let's just say that some people here didn't exactly make the Ramseys feel welcome at first, but things are improving. Jessi is adjusting — and she's a great addition to our club!

So. These complicated people are the "little friends" Charlie mentioned. The more I thought about them, the more I looked forward to seeing them. I always look forward to club meetings.

When Charlie pulled into Claudia Kishi's

driveway (our meetings are always held in Claud's room) I leaped out of the car. I couldn't wait to get things started.

" 'Bye, Charlie!" I called to him. "Thanks! See you in half an hour!"

" 'Bye, kiddo. Have fun!"

Have fun? No problem! We always do.

CHAPTER 2

"Claud? Is that you?" I asked.

Claudia's grandmother Mimi had let me in and told me to go up to Claudia's room. So I had — and now all I could see was a pair of legs sticking out from behind an armchair.

"Yeah, it's me," said a muffled voice.

"What are you doing?" I asked.

"Looking for my Cheese Doodles. I know they're around here somewhere . . . but not under this chair, I guess. Look what I did find, though."

Claudia's legs disappeared. A hand clutched the back of the chair. Then she stood up. She was holding a paintbrush. "I've been looking for this. I wonder how it got under the chair. But where are the Cheese Doodles?"

I giggled. Claud is just like a squirrel. She hides food — then forgets where she hid it.

"I'll look under your bed for you," I volunteered.

I flopped onto my stomach, scrunched underneath the bed, and poked around in the art supplies Claudia keeps there. "Jackpot!" I exclaimed. "Here are the Cheese Doodles *and* a whole pack of those mini candy bars."

"Oh, goody!" said Claud. Even though our meetings are held just before dinner, Claudia always provides us with snacks, since we're starving by five-thirty. Well, she provides most of us with snacks. Dawn won't touch much of Claud's junk food.

"Hi, you guys!" Mary Anne came in just as I was crawling out from under the bed. "I brought Tigger over. I hope you don't mind. He needed a change of scenery." Mary Anne set her gray kitten on the floor. Tigger immediately found a piece of ribbon and began batting it around.

Dawn and Mal showed up next, and Jessi appeared last. She usually does. She's very busy in the afternoons, between ballet classes and a steady sitting job.

My friends were all crawling around on the floor playing with Tigger, so I called the meeting to order.

"Any club business?" I said loudly.

At the sound of my voice, everyone scrambled to their usual places — Claudia, Mary Anne, and Dawn on Claudia's bed, and Mal and Jessi on the floor. I always sit in Claud's director's chair. And I wear a visor.

I am the president and I must look like I mean business.

"The treasury is getting low," spoke up Dawn, our treasurer. "But when I collect dues next week, I think we'll be okay."

Maybe I better stop for a moment and tell you how our club runs.

As I've said, I'm the club president. This is because the idea for the club was mine. I got it way back at the beginning of seventh grade when my mom and my brothers and I were still living next door to Mary Anne. Mom was just getting to know Watson then. Anyway, one evening, Mom realized she needed a sitter for David Michael. Sam and Charlie and I were all going to be busy. So Mom had to find someone else. I watched her make call after call. And as I was watching, it occurred to me that Mom could save herself a lot of time if she could call one number and reach several sitters at once.

That was it! A brilliant idea! I did some baby-sitting in my neighborhood then. So did Mary Anne and Claudia. We decided to start a baby-sitting club. We also decided we should have a fourth member. That was when Claudia introduced us to Stacey McGill, a new friend of hers who had moved to Stoneybrook from New York City. Stacey had lots of experience and was a terrific sitter, too. We asked her to join us, we began advertising, and just like that we had a baby-sitting business.

We decided that if we were going to be serious about our business, then we had better run it professionally. First, we agreed to hold regular club meetings three times a week. We told our clients they could reach us at Claudia's number on Mondays, Wednesdays, and Fridays from five-thirty until six. (Claudia has her own phone and personal, private phone number.) One of us was certain to be free to take any job that came in.

Then we voted ourselves officers of the club.

I was made the president . . . for obvious reasons.

Claud was made the vice-president, since we would always be meeting in her room and using her phone. Plus, people would probably be calling the club number even when we weren't meeting, and Claudia would have to deal with that extra work.

Mary Anne, who's the neatest and most organized of the four original club members, was named secretary. Boy, does she have a lot of work to do. It's her job to line up sitting appointments, to keep all our schedules straight (such as when Claudia goes to art lessons or when Jessi has ballet classes), and to keep the club record book up to date. The record book is crucial (that's a really good word, meaning 'very, very important') to the running of the club. In it, Mary Anne keeps track of all our clients and their addresses and phone numbers. And on the appointment calendar pages she schedules our sitting jobs. (The treasurer also uses the record book, but I'll get to that in a minute.) Mary Anne is a wonder. I don't think she's slipped up yet. None of us has ever been booked for two jobs at the same time or anything like that.

Last but not least, we made Stacey McGill our treasurer. It was her job to keep track of how much money each of us earns (just for our own information), to mark it down in the record book, and to collect dues for our treasury. What do we use our treasury money for? Two main things. 1. Entertainment, such as club sleepovers and pizza parties. 2. Funds for supplying our Kid-Kits.

The Kid-Kits were my idea. I thought that a good way to entertain the kids we sit for would be with a box of fun. So we each decorated a cardboard carton and filled it with our old games, books, and toys. Then we bought some stuff like coloring books, activity books, and

15

crayons. We take the Kid-Kits on our sitting jobs so the kids can play with them and not be bored. We use the treasury money to replace things that get used up.

How did Dawn, Jessi, and Mal join the club? Well, Dawn joined not long after she moved here from California. She and Mary Anne had become friends quickly, our business was growing, and we needed extra help. So Dawn became our alternate officer. That meant that she could take over the duties of any other member if someone had to miss a meeting. That didn't last long, though. Unfortunately, Stacey had to move back to New York City. (This was *especially* unfortunate since she and Claudia had become best friends, and now they really miss each other.)

Anyway, after Stacey left, two things happened. Dawn became our new treasurer — and we realized we needed lots more help. Our club was doing a ton of business. (Don't get me wrong. I'm not complaining. But we did have a problem.) We'd already signed up two associate members, kids who don't come to meetings, but who are good sitters we can call on in a pinch. They are Shannon Kilbourne, who lives across the street from me in my new neighborhood — and Logan Bruno, Mary Anne's boyfriend! But they weren't enough.

16

We needed a regular member to replace Stacey. My friends and I thought and thought. We liked Mallory Pike, whom we already knew is good with kids, even if she is younger than the rest of us, but the problem was that her parents don't allow her to sit at night, except at her own house. Finally, we took on Mal *and* her friend Jessi. We figured that if they could take over a lot of our afternoon jobs, the rest of us could handle the nighttime stuff. So far, it's working just fine. Jessi and Mal are our junior officers.

There's one other thing I better tell you about — our club notebook. The notebook is different from the record book. It's a sort of journal. We're all responsible for writing up every single job we go on. Then, once a week, we're supposed to read about the jobs in the notebook. It's really helpful. We can find out if the kids we sit for are having problems the rest of us should know about, or how one of us sitters handled a sticky situation, and other important things, like if any kid has food allergies or special fears. The notebook was my idea and I know it was a good one. I also know that most of the other club members think writing in it is a big bore. Well, too bad. Writing in the book is one of our few club rules.

"Okay," I said, from the director's chair, "the treasury is in good shape. Anything else?"

"Aw, look at Tigger!" Dawn said suddenly. Tigger was sitting in one of Claudia's shoes, which was pretty cute — but I was trying to conduct a meeting.

"Anything besides Tigger?" I said sternly.

Five heads snapped to attention. And just then the phone rang. I was nearest to it, so I answered it. "Hello, Baby-sitters Club. . . Hi, Mrs. Rodowsky." (I heard Dawn groan, and I waved my hand at her to make her quiet down.) "Tuesday?" I repeated. "Okay, I'll get back to you . . . Yes . . . Okay, good-bye."

I hung up. Mary Anne had opened the record book to the appointment pages. "This coming Tuesday?" she asked.

I nodded.

"Let's see. You're free, Kristy, and so are you, Dawn."

"You can have the job, Kristy," said Dawn quickly.

I grinned wickedly. "Is Jackie too much for you?" I asked.

"Nooo. Not exactly. You know I like him. His brothers, too. It's just . . . Well, you never know what's going to happen at the Rodowskys'."

That's true. And it's all because of Jackie,

the middle of the three Rodowsky boys. Shea is nine, Archie is four, and Jackie is seven — and a walking disaster. He's just totally accident-prone. And he doesn't have little accidents like skinned knees. No, he's more apt to lock himself in the bathroom and then get his hand caught down the drain of the tub. I could understand why Dawn preferred not to sit for him.

"Schedule me for Tuesday," I told Mary Anne. Then I called Mrs. Rodowsky back to tell her that I would be sitting.

I had just hung up when the phone rang again. Then four more times. For quite awhile, all we could do was schedule jobs, although Claudia did manage to pass around the Cheese Doodles and little candy bars.

The meeting was almost over when Mary Anne suddenly said in a sort of strangled voice, "Uh, where's Tigger, you guys?"

We searched Claud's room from top to bottom. We found a bag of Doritos, a box of Mallomars, some Gummi Bears, and a package of Twinkies — but no Tigger.

Mary Anne was just beginning to get tearful when we heard someone say, "Perhaps you are looking for this."

Standing in Claud's doorway was her sister Janine, cradling Tigger. "I found him sitting on my computer," she said. She was trying to look cross, but you could tell she wanted to smile.

Mary Anne greeted Tigger as if he'd been missing for a year or so, and then the meeting ended.

Jackie Rodowsky, I thought as Charlie drove me home. Would my afternoon with the walking disaster be fun . . . or, well, a disaster?

CHAPTER 3

"Hit it! . . . Hit it! . . . No, *hit* — Oh, never mind," said Max Delaney crossly.

"Don't yell at me!" retorted his sister.

"Anyway, *you* never hit the ball," Karen accused Max.

Max stuck his tongue out at Karen, and Karen stuck hers out at Max.

It was Saturday, the day after our club meeting, and it was a gorgeous afternoon. I was baby-sitting for Karen, Andrew, and David Michael. We were in the backyard and a bunch of kids had come over to play softball . . . or to try to play softball. Amanda and Max Delaney were there (Amanda is eight and Max is six), and Linny and Hannie Papadakis had come over, too. Linny is David Michael's good friend, and Hannie is one of Karen's best friends. The girls are in the same class at school.

The kids had a pretty pathetic game going. Most of them were old enough to be in Little

21

League or to play T-ball, but I could see why they hadn't bothered to join a team. They all worked and worked and worked — and nothing happened. I'd never seen so many kids play ball so hard with so few results.

Hannie really couldn't hit. She never connected with the ball. Max dropped or missed every ball he tried to catch. David Michael was simply a klutz. He tripped over his feet, the bat, even the ball, and no matter how he concentrated, he somehow never did anything right, except pitch. Karen wasn't a bad hitter. And Andrew might have been a good catcher if he weren't so little, but he's only four, so balls went sailing over him right and left, even when he stretched for them. Amanda and Linnie were no better than the others.

"You guys," I said to the kids, "come over here for a sec, and let me help you get organized. I'll give you some pointers, too, okay?" (I happen to like sports a lot.)

Karen, Andrew, David Michael, Hannie, Linny, Max, and Amanda dropped their gloves, bats, and the ball. They gathered around me.

"First of all," I said, "Hannie, it helps to watch the *ball* when you're trying to hit it. Don't look away from it, even to look at your bat."

"Yeah," said David Michael knowingly, as

if I hadn't just told him the same thing the day before.

"And Max, the trick for holding onto the ball after you catch it is to close your glove around it right away. Otherwise, the ball will fall out. And keep your eye on the ball when you're trying to catch it, just like when you're trying to hit it. Don't look at your mitt or the batter. Got it?"

The kids nodded.

Then Andrew said, "What about me? I could catch those balls if I were taller."

"I know you could," I replied. "So let's work on your hitting and pitching instead. The only way to make you taller is to give you stilts. Or else hold up this game for a year or two while you grow."

Andrew giggled.

I divided the kids into teams — the four younger kids *versus* the three older ones. "Now!" I cried. "Let's play ball!"

David Michael pitched to Hannie. Hannie swung her bat. She missed the ball by about two feet. Three times. He pitched to Karen. Karen hit the ball. *Smack!* It sailed right to Amanda, who appeared to be looking at the ball — until just before it reached her glove. Then she glanced at her glove to see how things were going. The ball flew over her head.

Everyone groaned. Even Karen, who was running bases.

I gathered the kids around me again. "We're going to stop the game," I announced, "and have a softball clinic instead."

"Clinic?" repeated Amanda nervously. "You mean, like a hospital?"

"No. No, I mean when I work with each of you on your weak points — the stuff you need help with. I'll be your coach and trainer."

The kids looked excited. And David Michael said, "If I were in Little League, there'd be a coach to help me all the time."

"You should join," I told him. "The rest of you should, too. Or play T-ball."

"I can't," said Andrew. "I'm not old enough."

"I can't either," said Karen and Hannie.

"Why not?" I asked. "Girls can play."

"Yeah," said Karen, "but no one would want me."

"Or me," said Hannie.

"Or me," said Linny, David Michael, and Max.

"I don't want to join," announced Amanda. "I don't like playing ball *that* much."

"Well, the rest of us do," said Hannie, who does not get along with Amanda and probably never will.

"We want to be on a team," added David

Michael. "We just don't want to embarrass ourselves."

"No Little League?" I asked, knowing what the answer would be.

"Nope," he replied, and the other kids agreed with him.

Then Amanda spoke up. "Hey, Kristy, do you know Bart Taylor? He coaches his own team right here in the neighborhood. A whole bunch of kids belong. His team is called Bart's Bashers."

"Maybe we could join!" exclaimed David Michael.

"I could talk to Bart," I said slowly. "Where does he live, Amanda? And who is he, anyway?"

"He's this kid. He goes to Stoneybrook Day School. I think he's in eighth grade, just like you, Kristy." Amanda told me where he lives, which isn't too far from my house.

Well, I thought, I could go talk to him. I wouldn't like it — but I would do it. Why wouldn't I like it? A lot of reasons. For one thing, you can never tell about eighth-grade boys. Half of them are normal, the other half are jerks. And in this neighborhood, about half of both groups are also snobs. I figured my odds. I had a twenty-five percent chance of getting a plain jerk, a twenty-five percent chance of getting a snobby jerk, a twenty-five percent chance of getting a plain snob, and a twenty-five percent chance of getting a regular, old nice guy.

The odds were not great, but I would risk them.

If only my brothers and I went to private school like the rest of the kids in this neighborhood, then the kids wouldn't have to lord their snobbishness over us. On the other hand, we might be jerks ourselves then, and besides, I wouldn't be in the same school with Claudia, Mary Anne, Dawn, Jessi, and Mal.

Mom and Watson came home at three-thirty that afternoon. At four o'clock, I put Shannon on her leash and walked her over to Bart's house.

A very, very, very cute guy was in the Taylors' yard, raking up dead grass and twigs and things. It couldn't be Bart. Most people around here have gardeners to take care of their lawns.

The boy saw me slow down and look curiously at him.

"Can I help you?" he called.

"I'm, um, I'm looking for Bart Taylor," I replied.

"Well, you found him." Bart grinned.

I grinned back. So far, so good. Maybe Bart was from that normal nonjerky twenty-five percent.

Bart dropped his rake and crossed the yard to the sidewalk. "That's a great-looking dog," he said, as Shannon put her front paws on his knees and wagged her tail joyfully.

"She's a Bernese mountain dog," I told Bart. "Oh, my name's Kristy Thomas. I came by . . . I came by to ask you something."

Why did I feel so nervous? I've talked to boys before. I've been to dances with boys. I've been to parties with boys. But none of them had looked at me the way Bart was looking at me just then — as if standing on the sidewalk was a glamorous movie star instead of plain old me, Kristy Thomas. And, to be honest, none of them had been quite as cute as Bart. They didn't have his crooked smile or his deep, deep brown eyes, or his even, straight, perfect nose, or his hair that looked like it might have been styled at one of those hair places for guys — or not. I think it's a good sign if you can't tell.

"Yes?" said Bart, and I realized I'd just been staring at him.

"Oh. Oh," I stammered. "Um, what I wanted to ask you is, well, I heard about your softball team, and I wondered whether you need any more players.''

Bart laughed. ''You're a little old,'' he replied.

''Oh, it's not me!'' I cried. ''It's my younger brother, and my little stepbrother and stepsister, and, let's see, one, two, three other kids. My stepbrother, Andrew, is only four,'' I rushed on. ''I feel I have to tell you that. And none of them is very good. Well, Karen's not a bad hitter, but David Michael's a klutz, and Linny's — ''

''Whoa!'' exclaimed Bart. ''Hold it. You're talking about six kids? I could take on one more, *may*be two, but not six. I've already got more kids than I need.''

Bart and I talked a little while longer. I decided two things. Since Bart couldn't handle any more kids, I would start my own team. I would take on any kid who really wanted to play on a team, no matter how young or klutzy or uncoordinated he or she was. I would call the other girls in the club and tell them to keep their ears open for kids who'd want to join. Maybe Jamie Newton, or some of the Pikes or Barretts would be interested. I could talk to Watson about the team. Watson loves baseball. In all honesty, he's not the most athletic person I can think of, but he's a huge baseball fan, and he's good at organizing and running things — even better than I am, and I don't mind admitting it. If I wanted to start a softball team, Watson was the person to go to.

The other thing I decided was that I had a Gigantic Crush on Bart Taylor.

CHAPTER 4

Monday

This afternoon I baby-sat for Myriah and Gabbie Perkins. What can I say? We always have a good time together. If Kristy had to move away, and a new family had to move into her house, I'm glad my dad and I got the Perkinses as our new neighbors.

Anyway, I guess I'm off the subject. Our afternoon went great, of course. And I got some kids for Kristy's ball team, but you already know that, Kristy, since I called you as soon as I finished sitting. What happened was that when Mrs. Perkins left, Jamie Newton and Nina Marshall showed up to play with Gabbie and Myriah.

30

Things got sort of out of hand, so I suggested playing catch in the backyard....

R*owf! Rowf! Rowf!*

"Hey, is that you, Mary Anne?"

"Toshe me up, Mary Anne Spier!"

The door to the Perkinses' house hadn't even opened and already there was happy noise and commotion as the girls and Chewy clamored for Mary Anne. The Perkins girls are Myriah, who's five and a half, Gabbie, who's two and a half, and Laura, the new baby. Chewy (short for Chewbacca) is the Perkinses' big, friendly, black Labrador, a great dog, even if he is sort of, well, high-spirited.

Myriah was the one calling, "Is that you?" She knows she's supposed to find out who's at the door before she opens it, even if her mother or father is home. Gabbie was the one calling, "Toshe me up." That's her way of saying, "Pick me up and give me a hug, please." No one knows where that phrase came from. She just invented it. And she almost always calls people (except her sisters and parents) by their full names.

31

"Yes, it's me! It's Mary Anne!" Mary Anne replied.

The door was flung open. There were Chewy, Myriah, and Gabbie in an excited bunch on the other side of the screen door. Mary Anne let herself in, and Myriah threw her arms around Mary Anne's legs in a happy hug. She and Mary Anne have been special friends ever since Mary Anne showed her how they could look out their bedroom windows and see each other, just like she and I used to do. (Myriah's room is my old room.)

Even with Chewy barking and leaping around, and Myriah gripping her legs, Mary Anne leaned over to toshe Gabbie up.

"Look, Mary Anne Spier," said Gabbie, holding out her finger. On the finger was a Band-Aid with pictures of Baby Kermit printed all over it. "I have an owie," she informed her sitter.

"An owie!" exclaimed Mary Anne. "Oh, no. How did that happen?"

"I was playing, and by accident, my finger went *WHAM* on the side of the TV. I was running, and it just went *WHAM!*"

"It's only a little owie," added Myriah, looking up at Mary Anne and Gabbie.

"No, it's a big one."

"No, little. How could — "

"Girls!" called Mrs. Perkins. "Let me talk to Mary Anne for a moment."

Mrs. Perkins came down the stairs with Laura bundled up in a baby blanket. Us sitters would love to take care of Laura sometimes, but she's just too little. Mrs. Perkins usually takes her wherever she goes. I guess one baby is a lot easier than one baby plus two kids.

Mrs. Perkins made sure that Mary Anne knew where the emergency numbers were, where she was going, and when she'd be back. Then she left. She hadn't been gone long when the doorbell rang.

"I'll get it," said Mary Anne. "You guys hold Chewy."

Chewy just loves to gallumph up to visitors. All he wants to do is greet them, but sometimes people don't know that. The sight of a huge dog running straight at you can be scary, especially if you're only four or five years old and not much taller than Chewy.

Mary Anne opened the door. There were Jamie Newton and Nina Marshall. They're both kids in the neighborhood and they're both four years old. Jamie was no surprise, but Nina sort of was. Our club sits for Jamie all the time, and for Nina and her little sister Eleanor sometimes, too, but while Nina hardly ever goes to the Perkinses', Jamie often does.

Mary Anne was glad to see both of them, though.

"Hi, you guys!" she said. "Did you come over to play?"

"Yup," said Jamie and Nina at the same time.

Mary Anne had just let them in and closed the front door when she heard a *rowf!* Chewy had struggled out of Myriah and Gabbie's grasp. He made a skidding dash through the hallway. Mary Anne caught him and led him out into the fenced-in backyard. Chewy is a handful — a happy handful with a doggie grin.

When Mary Anne went back in the house, she found things a little out of hand. Nina was running after Myriah with a giant foam-rubber banana. "Zonk! Zonk! Zonk!" she kept crying as she hit Myriah over the head with it.

Gabbie had found a plastic pitcher from her tea set. She had filled it with water and was carrying it through the house, crying, "Drinks for sale! Drinks for sale! Who wants to buy special water?"

"I do!" Jamie replied. "How much does it cost?"

"Four hundred dollars."

"Okay." Jamie reached into his pocket. He pretended to give Gabbie some money.

"Thank you," she said. Then she handed

34

Jamie the water and he drank it right out of the pitcher.

"Mmm, yummy. May I have — "

"Zonk! Zonk!" cried Nina. She and Myriah were tearing toward Gabbie and Jamie and the pitcher. Every time Nina zonked Myriah, Myriah replied, "Boi-oi-oi-oing!"

"You guys!" Mary Anne said desperately. "Look out!"

Too late.

Myriah and Nina crashed into Jamie and Gabbie. Water splashed everywhere.

"I think," said Mary Anne, "that it's time to play outside. May I have the pitcher and the banana, please? And would the four of you clean up the water before you put your jackets on?"

Mary Anne had never seen so many paper towels used to clean up such a small puddle, but at least the mess got mopped up. Then she took the kids into the Perkinses' backyard.

"How about some catch?" she suggested, remembering my phone call about starting a softball team.

"With Chewy around?" replied Myriah. "We better put him inside."

"Oh, poor Chewy," said Mary Anne. "He'll miss out on the fun. Let's leave him outside for just a little while."

"Okay-ay," said Myriah in a singsong voice that clearly meant she thought Mary Anne's idea was not a very wise one.

The kids found two bats — a wiffle bat and a regular one; three balls — a wiffle ball, a softball, and a tennis ball; and a couple of mitts.

"I'll be the pitcher," Myriah announced. "Nina, you be in the outfield. Gabbie and Jamie, you're the batters. You're on the other team."

Mary Anne was impressed. Myriah seemed to know a lot about playing ball.

"Okay, here comes the ball!" Myriah announced to Jamie, who was ready with the bat.

Jamie took one look at the softball flying toward him, dropped the bat, put his hands over his head, and ducked.

Guess who caught the ball? Chewy. Everyone ran after him. Chewy had the time of his life. He loves games. But when the kids couldn't catch him, they gave up. Besides, it was Gabbie's turn at bat, and since she's so little, Mary Anne told Myriah she'd have to pitch the wiffle ball. Then she gave Chewy a rawhide bone to keep him busy while the kids played.

Myriah tossed the wiffle ball.

Whack! Gabbie hit it. She looked extremely

pleased with herself. But she just stood by home plate, holding the bat. "Now, what do I do?" she asked.

"Run, you dope!" exclaimed Nina.

"Nina, no name-calling," Mary Anne admonished her.

The kids barely heard Mary Anne. Myriah went after the ball, caught it, ran to home plate, where Gabbie was still standing, and tagged her sister. "You're out!" she cried.

Mary Anne told me later that the game went on in pretty much the same way the game at my house had gone. Jamie ducked all balls, whether he was supposed to be hitting them or catching them. Gabbie wasn't too bad at hitting and catching — but she didn't understand much concerning the game of softball. (What can you expect from a two-and-a-half-year-old?) Nina, like Hannie Papadakis, tried hard, but wasn't particularly coordinated. Then there was Myriah. She was actually a pretty good player.

"Why don't you try out for Little League?" Mary Anne wanted to know.

"Can't. I'm old enough for T-ball, but not Little League."

"Would you like to play on a real team?" Mary Anne asked.

"Sure!" replied Myriah, and Mary Anne was

surprised when the rest of the kids said, "Sure!" as well.

"Really?" she asked. "You too, Gabbers?"

Gabbie nodded solemnly.

"Well," said Mary Anne, and she told them about my softball team.

The kids were enthusiastic, especially Myriah. They spent the rest of the afternoon hitting balls (or ducking them) — and then rescuing them from the jaws of Chewbacca, who had long ago given up on the rawhide.

CHAPTER 5

I always step onto the Rodowskys' front porch with a feeling of trepidation. (I like the word *trepidation*. It means alarm or dread, but somehow it seems less awful than those words.) The reason for the trepidation is, well, you know — Jackie, our very own walking disaster. Things happen to him. Sometimes things just happen because he's *around*. Imagine Paddington Bear. Imagine the little girl Eloise from the book called *Eloise*. Then put all that energy and mischief inside a character as nice as Charlie Bucket from *Charlie and the Chocolate Factory*. That's Jackie Rodowsky.

Because Jackie is basically a nice kid, I like to sit for him. But because I never know what's going to happen, I feel that trepidation. I feel it the whole time I'm at the Rodowskys'. It comes over me as soon as I reach their house, and it leaves the moment my sitting job is over.

I rang the Rodowskys' bell.

Mrs. Rodowsky answered the door, gave me the usual instructions, and began to put her coat on.

"Where are the boys?" I asked.

Mrs. Rodowsky smiled. "They're in the rec room," she said, lowering her voice. "Peek down there."

I peeked. The room looked ready for a party. Streamers crisscrossed the ceiling, and bunches of balloons hung here and there. The boys were busy blowing up more balloons and opening packages of paper plates and cups and party favors.

"Aww," I said, smiling. "Whose birthday is it?"

"Bo's." Mrs. Rodowsky looked at me meaningfully.

"Bo's? . . . Oh, the dog's!" I giggled.

"He's two today, and the boys decided they wanted to give him a party. They've even wrapped up presents for him, and on my way home this afternoon, I'm supposed to pick up a birthday cake — a *small* one — with Bo's name on it. Can you believe it?"

"I think it's great!" I said. "We never did anything like that for our collie Louie, even though we loved him a lot. But maybe when our new puppy turns one, we'll have a party

40

for her. We'll even invite Bo, since he'll know how to behave at a dog party.''

Mrs. Rodowsky laughed. ''Well, I better get going. Let the boys do whatever they want for the party — within reason. Then take them outside for awhile.''

''Okay,'' I said. I walked Mrs. Rodowsky down the stairs to the rec room.

'''Bye, boys!'' she called as she left through the back door.

They barely heard her.

''So, you guys,'' I said, ''what did you get Bo for his birthday?''

All three boys looked at me in surprise.

''Where'd you come from?'' asked Shea, the nine-year-old.

''I've been here for about five minutes,'' I told him. ''Your mom just left. I know all about Bo's party. You look like you're doing a great job.''

''There's not much left to do,'' said Shea.

''Nope,'' agreed Jackie, who's seven. ''Just make the lemonade and find the birthday candles. And finish setting the table.'' Jackie glanced at a folding table that had been covered with a paper cloth. It looked like a table for a kid's birthday party.

''I'll find the candles!'' volunteered Archie, the four-year-old.

"I'll finish the table," said Shea.

"Then I guess I better make the lemonade," Jackie said, and added, "I'm making pink lemonade. It's more special."

"I'll help you!" I said quickly.

"*No!* I can do it myself. I'm not a baby."

"Okay, okay. Sorry."

This is what I mean by trepidation. I didn't want to hurt Jackie's feelings, but I knew (well, I was pretty sure) that letting Jackie make lemonade would lead to a disaster.

I let him do it anyway.

"It's just a mix," he said. "All you do is add water."

That didn't sound too dangerous. The one thing I insisted on, though, was a plastic pitcher. Letting him fill up something glass was plain foolish.

"Kristy? Can you help me look for the candles?" Archie said then. "Shea told me they're in a box in the basement, and, um, I don't want to go down there by myself."

"Sure," I replied. I held out my hand. "Come on, Red."

"Red!" exclaimed Archie. "That's not my name."

"Red is a nickname for anyone with red hair," I told him, "like you guys have." The

Rodowsky boys all have flaming red hair and plenty of freckles.

Archie and I left Jackie in the kitchen with the lemonade mix, and Shea in the rec room, setting the table. Hand in hand, we descended into the basement. I had to admit, the Rodowsky's basement *was* a little spooky.

We had just found the candles when, from above, we heard a *thunk* and a *whoosh*. Then we heard Jackie say, "Uh-oh."

Archie and I didn't waste a second. We ran up the stairs to the rec room and then to the kitchen. Shea was already there. He and Jackie were staring at a large pink puddle on the floor, and pink drips down the sides of the cabinets, the dishwasher, and the table and chairs. Jackie was blushing as red as his hair.

"It was an accident," he told me.

With Jackie, it's always an accident. And once he gets started, it's hard for him to stop. Have you ever heard the saying that "bad things happen in threes"? Well, with Jackie, they happen more like in fifteens.

"Come on, let's clean up," I said. I'd meant just for Jackie and me to clean up, but Shea and Archie pitched in, too. They're used to helping their brother out.

When the kitchen was clean and nonsticky

again, and another pitcher of lemonade had been made (we made it in the sink and *I* carried the pitcher to the refrigerator), I said, "Is everything ready for Bo's party now?"

"Yes," answered the boys.

"Good. Then we're going outside." I was not about to wait around for another disaster, and disasters were less apt to happen outside.

"What are we going to do?" asked Archie, as he and his brothers were putting on their jackets.

"*I* need to practice for Little League," said Shea importantly.

Of course, my ears pricked up at that. "Little League?" I repeated. "Jackie, are you in Little League, too?"

"Naw," said Jackie, staring at his feet.

Shea snorted rudely, but I ignored his behavior. "Go get your baseball equipment," I told him.

A few moments later, the Rodowsky boys were swinging bats, and tossing balls in the air. I was standing on a flat rock which Shea assured me was the pitcher's mound. "Okay, batter up!" I called.

"Me first! Me first!" cried Jackie. He leaped next to an old magazine (home plate).

I pitched the ball. It was a good pitch — I mean, an easy one. If I'd been pitching in a real game, it would have been like saying to the other team, "Okay, just go ahead and score yourself a run." But Jackie missed the ball. Not by much, though.

Archie missed my next easy pitch, too, but then he's only four, and also left-handed, which makes things a little more difficult.

Shea, on the other hand, slammed the ball so hard, and it traveled so far, that even Bo couldn't find it.

"Home run! Home run!" shouted Shea. He jumped gleefully up and down on the magazine.

"Kristy, Kristy, can I pitch now?" asked Jackie. "I want to try pitching."

"Good luck," Shea muttered sarcastically, but I was the only one who heard him.

Jackie took his place on the rock. He wound up his arm like professional ball players do. He threw straight to Shea — and somehow, somehow, the ball hit the house next door. Boing, boing, boing, slurp. It bounced down the roof and landed in a rain-filled gutter.

"Jackie!" exclaimed Shea.

"Oh, brother," I said. "Now we're going to have to go over there and tell your neighbors there's a softball in their gutter."

"Don't worry about it," said Shea. "Four others are there, too. Our dad's going over on

Saturday to get them out. He can just get this one while he's at it."

"Do you have another ball?" I asked.

"We'll use a tennis ball," said Jackie, heading for the garage. "I'll get it. I want to try batting again. I *know* I can hit the ball."

Jackie was a disaster on the ball field, just like he was anywhere else, but he was determined to play. And he did hit the ball from time to time. He reminded me of David Michael. I really admired him.

While Jackie was getting the tennis ball, we heard a huge crash in the garage. Since I was tired of disasters, all I said was, "Whatever it is, pick it up, Jackie!"

"Okay!" he shouted back.

Jackie returned with the tennis ball.

"Anything broken in there?" I asked.

"Nope."

A miracle.

Jackie handed the ball to Shea, who pitched it to him.

"Keep your eye on the ball!" I called.

Whack! Jackie slammed the ball. "I hit it!" he yelled, and made a dash for first base.

Shea caught it on the fly, but Jackie kept running. He ran all the way around the yard to home plate, where he was met by Shea. Shea held the tennis ball in Jackie's face. "Fly ball," he informed him. "You're out. Jackie, you will never be in Little League." He didn't have to add, "Because no one would want you," but that's what he meant, and we all knew it.

"Yes, I will," replied Jackie stubbornly. "I *will* be in Little League. I'll practice and practice. I'll get as good as you. I'll get *better* than you. I'll be the best player in the universe." Jackie punctuated his speech by tripping over his shoelace.

Sheesh. He's even worse than David Michael, I thought. But I was pretty sure I had a new member for my softball team. A few minutes later, I was positive. I noticed that the worse Jackie played, the harder he tried. He wouldn't give up. Maybe he just needed some confidence and coaching. Watson had said those things were very important. (Watson, by the way, had been extremely flattered when I'd gone to him about organizing a team. He had also been extremely helpful and extremely nice.)

I told Jackie about my softball team. Jackie's face lit up like candles on a birthday cake. I kind of wished Watson could have seen that smile.

That night I got some interesting phone calls.

The first was from Jessi Ramsey. "Guess what," she said. "Matt Braddock wants to be on your team."

"Great!" I exclaimed. Matt's a terrific kid and a terrific ball player — but he was born deaf. He can't hear or speak. You have to communicate with him using sign language. Luckily, a lot of the kids in Stoneybrook learned some sign language after they met Matt, so this isn't much of a problem.

Then Mallory called. "I talked to my brothers and sisters. Nicky, Claire, and Margo want to be on your team," she said. "I tried to talk Vanessa into it, but she's not interested. And the triplets are in Little League."

Next to call was Dawn, saying that two of the three Barrett kids she often sits for were interested, plus three friends of theirs (whom I didn't know).

The last call was from Claudia. "I haven't found a single kid for your team," she wailed.

"Don't worry about it," I told her. "I've got twenty already."

"Wow!"

"Yeah."

It was time for a planning session with Watson.

CHAPTER 6

Boy. I did not have any idea what I was getting myself into when I decided to coach a softball team, even after I talked to Watson. It seemed like such a nice thing to do — organize a team for kids who were too embarrassed or too young to be in Little League or to play T-ball. Well, it *was* a nice thing. I knew that. And Watson knew that, which was why he was so encouraging. But it was also . . . Well, you'll see what happened.

Anyway, as soon as I found out that twenty kids wanted to be on my team, I got to work. First, I made a few lists. The Baby-sitters Club is always doing this, and it's very helpful. One list, the most important, was of the names and ages of the kids on the team, and their special problems. It looked like this:

Gabbie Perkins - 2½ - doesn't understand game yet
Jamie Newton - 4 - afraid of the ball

Nina Marshall - 4 - probably just needs work
Andrew Brewer - 4 - just needs work
Suzi Barrett - 4 - ?
Myriah Perkins - 5 - ? (probably just needs work)
Claire Pike - 5 - ?
Patsy Kuhn - 5 - (haven't even met her)
Laurel Kuhn - 6 - (haven't even met her)
Karen Brewer - 6 - just needs work
Max Delaney - 6 - just needs work
Buddy Barrett - 7 - ?
David Michael Thomas - 7 - a klutz
Hannie Papadakis - 7 - poor hitter
Matt Braddock - 7 - excellent player; uses sign language
Jackie Rodowsky - 7 - a walking disaster
Margo Pike - 7 - ?
Nicky Pike - 8 - ?
Jacob Kuhn - 8 - (haven't even met him)
Linny Papadakis - 8 - just needs work

I looked at my list. I did a little math. The
average age of my team was 5.8 years — just
under six. These were *young* kids. Of course,
if they were older, they'd have joined Little
League. Well, some of them would have.

Then I made a list of questions to answer:

Where would we meet?
When and how often would we meet?

Would anyone help me?
What would be the purpose of my team?
Does Bart Taylor think I'm cute?

A zillion phone calls later, Watson and I had found answers to all but the last question. Thanks to Watson, we got permission to meet at the playground of Stoneybrook Elementary School. This was convenient since a lot of the kids lived nearby. We would meet on Tuesdays after school, and on Saturday afternoons.

Some of the club members volunteered to help me. Some of them also sounded pretty uncertain. For instance, Jessi said, "I'm a dancer, not an athlete. I barely know the difference between a football and a baseball." And Claudia said flat out, "I hate sports . . . but I'll help you." Mary Anne and Dawn were more helpful, and said, "We don't know much about sports, but we love the idea of your team. Just tell us how to help." Mallory was pure help: "I've lived with Little League for two seasons now. I know all there is to know about kids and ball games. I'll do anything — except watch Claire have a tantrum."

Tantrum? Uh-oh.

The purpose of the team? Watson and I talked about that for a long time, and Watson

51

did not say one jerky thing. We agreed that the purpose of the team was the reason I'd started it — to coach kids who wanted to improve their playing skills, but more importantly, just to have fun. I figured I could put the twenty kids on two sides each time we met, and we could have a game — after coaching. Coaching first, I decided, then a game. Maybe just a seven-inning game, or an even shorter one. Coaching (and I promised myself I would *never* lose my temper with any kid, no matter what) followed by a game should be a lot of fun.

Does Bart think I'm cute? Well, how would I know? Maybe the better question was, *Had* Bart thought I *was* cute? I hadn't seen him since I'd walked Shannon over to his house. And I'd probably never see him again, considering we went to different schools and had different friends. I tried to put Bart and my Gigantic Crush out of my mind.

That was not too difficult. On Saturday afternoon, we held our first team meeting. Every single kid showed up! So did Dawn and Mallory.

"Where'd you get all that equipment?" Dawn asked me in awe, as she looked at the things surrounding me — four bats, five mitts, a catcher's mask, a softball, and a wiffle ball (for Gabbie).

"Oh, it's all ours. With six kids in your family," (I count Andrew and Karen as part of my family, of course), "two of whom are guys in high school, you'd be surprised at what accumulates. Some of it's mine. The only thing we're low on is balls. All Sam and Charlie have are hardballs, and I couldn't find any tennis balls."

The twenty kids gathered around me eagerly. We were standing at the edge of the blacktopped part of the playground, near a four-square court. I saw that a few parents had come along, and I began to feel nervous. I felt like a teacher on her first day at school when some parents have stuck around to see how good she is. One of the mothers was Mrs. Braddock, and I knew she was just there to translate everything I said into sign language for Matt, but still. . . .

The kids were looking at me expectantly. I edged away from the blacktop and said, "Let's sit down. I want to talk to you for a few minutes."

The kids plopped down in the grass. Dawn and Mallory sat on either side of me. The parents hovered in the background (except for Mrs. Braddock).

"First," I said, "I just want to introduce myself to the three kids I don't know, the Barretts' friends." It was easy to spot them in the crowd. They were the only faces I didn't recognize.

I pointed to the oldest-looking one. "You must be Buddy's friend," I said. "I'm Kristy Thomas."

The boy nodded. "I'm Jacob Kuhn, but call me Jake. I'm eight," he added.

The other Kuhns turned out to be Laurel, who was six and so shy that Jake had to say her name and age for her, and Patsy, who was five, Suzi Barrett's friend.

"Well," I said, "I want you guys to know that we're here to play softball, but mostly we're here to have fun. I'm going to coach you and teach you skills during the first part of each afternoon, and then we'll divide into two teams and play a game. If you think you're not a good player, don't worry about it. There's no pressure here. This is *just fun*. Got it?"

I saw a few eyes light up, Jackie's among them.

David Michael raised his hand, just as if he were in school. "I'm a klutz," he said.

"I don't care," I replied. "Everybody here is good at some things and not so good at others."

Jamie Newton raised his hand. "I'm afraid of the ball," he admitted.

"I can never hit it," Claire Pike announced.

"Then those are the things we'll work on," I said, smiling. "Now. How many of you are friends with Matt Braddock?"

A few hands went up, including the Barretts' and the Pikes'.

"Matt is deaf," I explained to the others. "He can't hear and he doesn't talk. But I'll tell you something. He is one super ball player." (Matt beamed when his mother signed that to him.)

My stepsister Karen raised her hand. "We can talk to him, though," she informed everyone. "We can talk to him in his secret sign language, just like his mother is doing now."

"That's right," I agreed. "I'll show you the signs you need to know to play ball with Matt."

"I already know them!" said Nicky Pike proudly.

"Me too," said Buddy Barrett.

"Great. Now today, instead of having a practice first, I think we should just hold a game. I haven't seen many of you play, and — "

"Wait!" cried Jackie. "Don't we need a team

name? If we're going to be a ball team, we need a name like the Mets or the Dodgers or the Red Sox."

"Yeah!" cried all the kids.

Suddenly they were shouting out dozens of suggestions — the Stoneybrookers, the Tigers, the Big Leaguers. But when Jackie yelled out, "How about Kristy's Crushers?" everyone agreed.

"And we could spell 'Crushers' with a 'K'," added Margo Pike. "You know, to go with Kristy. Kristy's Krushers."

"No!" cried Karen. "That's wrong. That's not how you spell 'crushers.' You spell 'crushers' with a 'C'!" (Karen takes her spelling very seriously.)

But she was voted down. Every other kid liked "Kristy's Krushers-with-a-'K.' "

"And we should have team uniforms," added Jake Kuhn. "The kids in Little League do."

I hadn't thought about that. It seemed expensive. "Where will we get uniforms?" I wondered aloud. Even Watson hadn't thought of that.

"How about team T-shirts?" suggested Mallory, coming to my rescue. "If each of you could get a plain white T-shirt, you could iron on 'Kristy's Krushers.' You know, with those letters you get at Woolworth's."

56

This seemed to appease the kids, even though we all knew that T-shirts were not as good as real uniforms.

"Well," I said, "let's get a game going here. Everyone stand in a line."

It took a few moments, but the kids organized themselves into a long, straggly line.

"Now count off in twos," I instructed them. "One, two, one, two. . . ."

I gathered the Ones and the Twos. "These are your teams," I said. "We'll toss a coin to see which one is up at bat first. Then I'll assign positions to the rest of you."

The game began. Linny Papadakis was the pitcher.

He pitched to Claire, who missed the ball by a mile.

He pitched to Jamie Newton, who, at the last moment, dropped the bat, covered his head, and ducked.

I winced, then hoped that none of the kids had seen me.

Off in right field, I caught sight of Laurel Kuhn making a dandelion chain. "Hey, Laurel!" I yelled. "Watch the game, okay?"

Laurel nodded, but over in left field, Hannie Papadakis was looking for four-leaf clovers.

"Hannie! Heads up!"

"Left field is boring!" she replied.

Linny pitched the wiffle ball to Gabbie Perkins, who made the first hit of the game. She even ran for first base, but halfway there she got a case of the giggles, which slowed her down. The first basewoman caught the ball before Gabbie reached her.

Jackie was up at bat next. He got in the next hit of the game — right into the woods behind the school.

"Foul ball!" I cried.

Eight children went looking for the softball. They couldn't find it, and no one wanted to play with the wiffle ball.

"Game over," I announced.

"Thanks to Jackie," someone muttered.

But all I said was, "You guys were great! Keep up the good work. I'll see you on Tuesday."

" 'Bye, Coach!" called Linny Papadakis.

Coach? . . . Coach! I liked the sound of that.

I couldn't wait to tell Watson about our first practice. No one had cried or gotten hurt. The kids had been excited. They'd had fun. They'd come up with a team name. As far as I could tell, the practice had been a success.

monday

mallery! What a game!

I'll say, Claud. Kristy's Krushers are terrific. We hardly had to babbysit today.

Nope. We were fans instead.

Expect for that one tantrum.

Well, those are bound to happen every now and then. I warned Kristy about them. Claire may be silly, but she's also got a temper. Especially when she's doing something, you know...

Compertive?

Well, competitive. And only when it has to do with baseball....

Sometimes I think the Pikes are the best thing that ever happened to Matt Braddock and his nine-year-old sister Haley. When they moved to the Pikes' neighborhood, Haley thought it would be the end of the world. She thought that because Matt's deaf, kids would think he was weird — and if they thought he was weird, they would think *she* was weird, and that neither one would ever make new friends.

Luckily Haley was wrong, thanks to Jessi and Mallory. Jessi started bringing the Braddock kids over to Mallory's house, and Mallory and Jessi told the Pike kids that Matt knew a *secret language*. What a mystery! They all wanted to learn it, too. Now they can talk to Matt pretty well. If there's trouble, Haley helps out, since she can sign almost as well as she can speak. Plus, Haley has gotten to be friends with Vanessa, and Matt is friends with the Pike boys.

Anyway, on the day that Claud and Mallory were sitting for the seven other Pike kids, Jessi brought Matt and Haley over as usual. Claud and Mal were in the backyard with the Pike kids. It was a sunny day, and everyone felt like being outdoors. Margo was jumping rope on the patio, Vanessa was teaching Claire to play jacks, the triplets were trying to do acrobatics in the grass, and Nicky was examining a scab on his elbow.

"That drives me crazy," said Mal, watching the triplets. "They're going to break their backs or something. I just know it."

"Oh, they are not," said Claud. "How many times have you tried stuff like that?"

"Just once," replied Mal, "and I sprained my wrist."

"Oh."

Claudia was saved by a shout of, "Hi!"

Vanessa had spotted Jessi, Haley, and Matt. She left the jacks game and ran to them, waving to Matt. Waving is the sign for "Hi!" (Easy, huh?) Matt waved back, then joined the triplets. The triplets stopped fooling around (to Mallory's relief).

"Want to play ball?" they asked Matt with their hands.

Matt nodded vigorously.

"Can we play, too?" asked Claire. "Nicky and Margo and me? We're on a ball team now, you know. We're Kristy's Krushers, just like Matt."

Mallory could tell that her brothers wanted to snicker — obviously, they didn't think much of the Krushers — but they didn't want to hurt Matt's feelings.

"Hey!" Adam cried suddenly. "How about

Little Leaguers *versus* the Krushers? That would be an, um, interesting game."

"Oh, but it wouldn't be fair," spoke up Nicky. "There are only three of you guys . . . and four of us Krushers."

"Believe me, that'll be plenty fair," said Jordan snidely.

By that time, Matt was looking angry, as he often does when he's left out of a conversation. (It must be awfully frustrating.) Haley rushed over and signed to him. When Matt understood what was being planned, his face lit up. He signed furiously to his sister.

Haley burst out laughing. "Matt says the Krushers can beat the pants off you Little Leaguers!"

"Oh, yeah?" said Adam, leaning toward Matt menacingly.

No one needed to translate that, and Matt's response was to draw his finger across his throat, clearly meaning, "You *die!*" But he was smiling and so was Adam.

"Are we on?" said Byron.

Claire, Margo, Nicky, and Matt were facing the triplets. Their answer? *Yes!* And Claire added, "And we'll beat you, all right!"

"Oh, sure," said Jordan. "You know what Claire's batting average is? *Zero.* She has *never* hit a ball."

"But I've caught a lot of them," she pointed out.

Adam and Byron headed into the Pikes' garage and returned with some mitts, bats, and softballs.

"Because we're so nice," said Byron, "we'll let you Krushers be up at bat first." And he signed to Matt, "Your team first."

Matt nodded, looking as if he thought the triplets were making a big mistake.

The triplets held a conference to choose positions, while Nicky signed that Matt should be the first batter up. Matt nodded, all business.

Jordan was the pitcher. Adam and Byron were combination outfielders and basemen. Jordan stared at Matt. He shuffled his feet around and adjusted the brim of his cap, trying to look professional. Then — *zoom!* He threw a fastball.

Matt was ready. His eyes on the ball, he swung and connected. The ball sailed over Jordan's head.

"I've got it! I've got it!" shouted Adam. And he did have it — but not on the fly. He didn't get it to third base until just after Matt had slid in.

"Yea!" cheered Vanessa and Haley from the sidelines.

"All *right!*" shouted Nicky. "See what us Krushers can do?"

Matt grinned and waved his fist over his head in a silent cheer.

"I see what *Matt* can do," said Jordan, getting set to pitch. "Now I want to see what *you* can do, little bro."

What Nicky could do was strike out. He handed the bat to Margo. Margo took it, positioned herself in the batter's box and kept her eyes on Jordan. She concentrated so hard that she didn't even blink when Adam called out, "Hey Margo, you're gonna strike out!"

Or when Nicky retorted, "You guys must be pretty worried if you have to try to scare us."

Claud and Mal looked at Jessi and smiled.

The triplets shut up. And Margo kept her batting stance.

Jordan pitched.

Margo fouled the ball.

Jordan pitched again. Then seven more times.

Finally Jordan shrugged. Enough was enough. He let Margo walk to first base.

Claire's turn.

"It's the strike-out queen!" shouted Byron. But the Krushers didn't react, and Byron shut up.

"Come on, Claire," Nicky said seriously to

his sister. "One out. Runners at first and third. I know you've never hit the ball, but if you hit it now you could send Matt home."

Claire nodded.

"Good. I know you can do it," said Nicky.

On the sidelines, the baby-sitters smiled at each other again. Nicky was rarely so nice to his sisters. Usually he teased them with rude songs or played tricks on them or tried to gross them out.

"The Krushers stick together," Claudia commented.

And then Claire struck out.

"Whoa. Two outs. Tantrum time," muttered Mallory.

But nothing happened.

Nicky was up again. He swung and missed. Then he slammed the ball deep into left field. Matt ran home. Margo ran home. And Nicky reached second base before he realized he better not go any further.

The Krushers looked at each other proudly. Claudia told me later that the triplets seemed sort of awed. (And maybe just the teeniest bit proud.) To the Krushers' credit, they didn't gloat. I wish I'd been there. I would have been proud of them, too.

I would have been proud right up until what happened next.

Matt struck out, the triplets ran off the field — and Claire threw a tantrum. I'd never seen Claire throw a tantrum. I didn't even know she threw tantrums until Mallory mentioned it over the phone. But sure enough, as soon as her team had three outs, Claire clenched her fists, screwed up her face, and began screeching, "No fair! No fair! No fair!" until, according to Claudia, who got the job of calming her down, it sounded more like she was saying, "Nofe-air! Nofe-air! Nofe-air!"

"She only throws baseball tantrums," Mallory informed me later. "She does it with ball games on TV, too."

However, Claire got over her tantrum and Matt pitched to the triplets. They scored four runs in the first inning. In the second inning the Krushers scored zero runs and the triplets scored three more. By the end of the fifth inning, when Mrs. Pike came home, the triplets were ahead, sixteen to five.

But, with the exception of Claire's tantrum, the Krushers never once lost their patience or their courage. They did lose their concentration a few times, but what can you expect from 5.8-year-old kids?

When the game was over, Jordan actually said to Nicky and his sisters, "Good game, you guys." Then he remembered to sign for Matt. Matt grinned.

Haley, who had watched the entire game with Claudia, Mallory, Jessi, and Vanessa, just said, "Whew. That was amazing. There was no way they could beat the triplets — but they never gave up."

"Never," agreed the others.

When Mal and Claudia told me about the game later, I felt terrific. My team, my Krushers, had real spirit.

CHAPTER 8

"Claire, can you please get out of that tree? And Karen, stop teasing your broth — Jamie, what are you doing? Leave that bat alone. You're supposed to hit balls with it, not walk on it."

"I'm a tightrope walker, Coach." Jamie replied, but he stepped off the bat.

It was the beginning of another practice with the Krushers. I seemed to be having a little trouble getting everyone organized. Claudia was there, and she was supposed to be helping me, but she'd found some candy in the pocket of her jeans and was concentrating on unwrapping it. You could tell that the candy was much more interesting to her than softball.

I clapped my hands. Suddenly I felt like Mr. Redmont, my old teacher from seventh grade. He was always clapping his hands to get kids' attention.

"Hey, you guys!" I called. "Would you come

here, please. . . . PLEASE? . . . *Claudia.* I need help."

What was wrong with everybody? I thought these kids wanted to play ball so badly.

Claudia popped a piece of candy into her mouth and wandered over to me. "What do you want me to do?" she asked.

I could have been sarcastic, but I kept my temper. After all, the kids were nearby. I didn't want them to think I was an ogre.

"Just help me get them together. We need some practice time first."

"Come on, guys!" I called again. "Where's your Krushers spirit?"

Right away, the kids ran to me — except for Claire. She was stuck in the tree. Claudia had to lift her down.

Boy, all I had to say was "Krushers" and the kids jumped to attention.

I began assigning tasks. "Jamie," I said, "I know you're a little afraid of the ball. Can you *throw* it, though?"

He nodded.

"Great. I want you to pitch to Claire for awhile. She needs practice hitting the ball." And, I thought, if she actually did hit it, Jamie might try to catch it. (Either that, or he would duck it.)

"Okay," said Claire and Jamie.

"David Michael and Nicky, I want you to work on your pitching. You guys just toss the ball to each other, okay?"

"Yup," they replied.

This time I was prepared with more equipment. I'd asked the kids to bring along some of their own stuff so they would have enough to practice with.

Our afternoon got underway. I'd assigned each Krusher something to work on, and I walked around and gave the kids pointers.

"Hannie, run toward the ball," I shouted. "Don't wait for it to come to you. You have to go after it. . . . Claire, keep your eye on that ball. . . ."

I almost shouted Matt's instructions to him, too, before I remembered that he wouldn't hear me. I signed to him instead, and he looked confused. I'd probably just told him to go price an elephant or something. I wished Haley or Mrs. Braddock or Jessi were there to help.

Claudia looked bored. She sat down in the grass and ate another piece of candy. Then she examined her fingernails.

"Time for a manicure?" I asked her.

Claud jumped. "Oh, sorry," she said.

"Listen, could you toss the ball to Jamie for awhile?" I asked her. "You're good with him," (it never hurts to flatter people), "and I'll work with Claire. They're not getting much accomplished together."

Claire was singing "I'm a Little Teapot" to Jamie, and every time she got to the part about "tip me over and pour me out" she released the softball from her underarm, which Jamie thought was hysterical.

I let practice go on for about ten more minutes. Then I called, "Game time!"

What a reaction! The kids jammed themselves around me. I had them count off in twos again, and as soon as the sides were organized, we got a game going. Right away, the kids were all business. Karen was the catcher for her side. She crouched behind home plate, wearing her mask and slamming one hand into her glove. "Attaboy! Attaboy!" she kept shouting, no matter what was going on.

I let David Michael pitch. First up at bat was Matt Braddock. He swung the bat and fouled. David Michael, who barely knows any sign language, signed something that looked like "monkey." Then he remembered a softball sign, but it was the one for "safe." It took ages to get everything sorted out.

When the first half of the inning was over, which was pretty soon (since after Matt was up, the next three hitters each struck out), I let our walking disaster go to bat first. He hit the ball and ran to second! While Linny Papadakis was at bat, Jackie stole third base. Then Myriah Perkins got in a single, Jackie ran for home, tripped over his feet, and was tagged out, just inches from the base.

"Darn, darn, double, double darn!" he shouted.

The other kids laughed, but not rudely.

At the start of the second inning, I let Jackie be the catcher. Like Karen, he loved wearing the mask and mitt. You could tell he felt professional.

Buddy Barrett was pitching now. He pitched to Jamie. Jamie concentrated, tried not to look scared, and ducked at the last minute. The ball slammed into Jackie's mouth.

"Jackie!" I cried. "What happened to the mask? You were just wearing it."

"I had to take it off, Coach," he replied. "I got my gum stuck on it. I wanted to see if I could make it look like a waffle by pressing it against the mask. You know, like you can do with Silly Put — Uh-oh!"

"What?" I asked.

"My mouth's bleeding! I think I knocked out my tooth. . . . No, it's just loose. Very loose."

I may make comments about food to gross out my friends, but I'll tell you one thing that grosses *me* out: very loose teeth. Especially bloody ones.

Claudia knows that. She stepped over to look in Jackie's mouth. "It's so loose it could practically fall out," she said. "Do you want me to pull it for you, Jackie? I've got a Kleenex right here."

Oh, oh, ew.

"All right," agreed Jackie.

The entire team crowded around to watch the proceedings. Not me, though. I stood as far away as possible. I pretended to check on our equipment.

A few minutes later, I saw the kids disperse. Jackie held up a tissue. "My tooth's in here, Coach!" he announced. He ran over to me and smiled a gap-toothed, slightly bloody smile. "I just love losing teeth."

Ew. I never liked losing teeth. I'm glad I'm past that stage. "Put the Kleenex and your tooth in your pocket," I told Jackie.

We played another inning, and I must say that everybody played harder than before. The kids *tried* hard, too, just like Mallory and Claudia said the four Krushers had done in the game against the triplets.

But it was getting late.

"I think this game is over," I said at the end

of the inning. "How many of you guys have bought T-shirts and iron-on letters?"

Most of the kids raised their hands.

"Good," I told them. "Try to wear your shirts to our next practice. Then we'll really look like a team, and everyone will know we're the Krushers."

The kids began to leave. Charlie arrived to pick up Karen, Andrew, David Michael, and me, and take us to our homes. (Karen and Andrew were going to their mom's house.) After they'd been dropped off, I began to daydream. I daydreamed about Bart. I'd been doing that a lot lately.

An idea came to me.

"Hey, David Michael," I said, "want me to walk Shannon for you tonight?"

David Michael loves Shannon, but he also loves getting out of his chores.

"Sure!" he replied. Then he narrowed his eyes. "What do I have to do for you?" he asked suspiciously.

Do for me? I hadn't thought about that, but what an opportunity.

"Umm . . ." I replied slowly, "learn five signs you need to know to play ball with Matt Braddock. Call Nicky Pike and ask him for help, okay?"

"Okay!"

David Michael thought he'd gotten the better part of the deal, but I knew that (with any luck) *I* had.

When supper was over that night, I found Shannon in the den, chewing on a rubber toy that looked like a steak.

"Want to go for a W-A-L-K?" I asked her.

We started spelling *walk* so Shannon wouldn't get all excited and think she was going out every time she heard the word. But we spelled it so often that Shannon has figured out what *W-A-L-K* means.

She abandoned the toy, leaped to her feet, and bounded to the back door, where I clipped on her leash. Then I told Mom and Watson that I was going to walk Shannon, and I set off. I wasn't *just* walking Shannon, though. I was walking Shannon by Bart Taylor's house. Pretty clever, huh?

I thought so. So I was totally surprised when, only halfway over there, who should I see coming toward me, but Bart! He was walking a rottweiler on this chain that could have tethered a lion. (In case you don't know, a rottweiler is your basic, gigantic dog. Next to Bart's dog, Shannon looked like a mouse.)

Bart and I spotted each other at the same time and called, "Hi!" Then we both slowed down. We weren't sure how our dogs would behave.

"This is Twinkle," Bart said. "He looks fierce, but he wouldn't hurt a flea."

"And Shannon," I replied, "won't believe that Twinkle wouldn't hurt a flea . . . but let's see what happens."

Poor Shannon approached Twinkle with her tail tucked between her legs. The dogs circled each other and sniffed, and Shannon discovered she was so little she could walk right under Twinkle, which Bart and I thought was pretty funny. When we realized that the dogs were going to be okay, we stood there on the sidewalk as night fell, and began to talk.

I told Bart how the Krushers were doing.

Bart laughed.

"What?" I asked.

"I don't believe it. My team's called the Bashers. The Bashers and the Krushers!"

It *was* funny.

Then I said, "Have you ever run into a kid who's afraid of balls and ducks them?"

Bart looked thoughtful. "I don't think so. But most of my kids are a little older than yours. They're about seven to nine. They're pretty much past being afraid of the ball and stuff. They're not great players, but they aren't babies."

"The Krushers aren't babies!" I cried.

Bart flushed. "Lighten up," he said. "I didn't really mean that. I was just pointing out that the Bashers are older."

"Sorry," I said, and then practically melted as the streetlights came on and caught Bart's hair, giving it a sort of glow.

Bart was the cutest guy I had ever seen.

"Hey," said Bart, "I've got an idea. Just to show you that I think your team is as good as mine, even if the kids are younger, how about a game? Bart's Bashers challenge Kristy's Krushers."

A game? A real game? Against Bart's team? I didn't know if the Krushers were ready for something like that, but I wasn't about to say no. I couldn't let Bart think I was afraid of his team. Besides, if we set up a game, I'd be sure to see him again — soon.

"Sure," I replied. "How about two weeks from Saturday? Is that enough time for the Bashers to get ready?"

"Of course! But what about the Krushers?"

"Oh, they'll be ready."

I grinned at Bart and he grinned back.

As I walked Shannon home a few minutes later, I felt as if there were cotton balls under my feet instead of concrete. And I'm sure my eyes were shining.

CHAPTER 9

Saturday

Wow! The Krushers are something else, Kristy. I'm really glad I got to sit for the Barretts on a practice day. Buddy and Suzi were so excited. They loved everything about being on the team, especially their T-shirts. They didn't even mind that it was on the chilly side today and they had to wear their team shirts over other shirts.

What can I say about this afternoon? It was great. Easiest sitting job I ever had. All I had to do was walk the kids to practice and back, and entertain Marnie while practice was going on. Marnie was in a good mood, so entertaining her was no problem. Plus she fell asleep for awhile. It's too bad about what Jackie did, but Buddy and Suzi were still excited as we walked back home later....

Boy. Thanks to me, Jessi really did have an easy sitting job. But I'm not complaining. After all, coaching a softball team was my idea. Jessi couldn't help it if Buddy and Suzi were on the team.

I have to admit that Jessi saw an unusual practice, though. I mean, a more exciting one than most. The kids gathered at the playground right on time — and every last one of them was wearing a Kristy's Krushers T-shirt, even the kids who hadn't yet bought shirts and letters when I'd asked about that before. I was wearing a Krushers shirt, too. After all, I was the coach.

You could almost *taste* the excitement in the air.

I got to the playground early. Watson had driven David Michael and me over and was going to stay to watch the practice. He headed for the stands, saying he would keep out of our way.

David Michael beamed as he helped me check the equipment. "We're a *real* team now," he said at least three times. "And everyone will know you're our coach. I like that. Red letters."

It was true that my shirt was lettered in red while the kids' shirts were lettered in black, but I was hoping a few other things might be clues that I was coach — like, I was thirteen instead of 5.8, and taller than the players.

The kids began to show up, all wearing T-shirts over sweat shirts or other shirts since it was a cool day.

"Hi-hi!" called Jamie, arriving with Gabbie, Myriah, and Mr. Perkins.

"Look at us, Coach!" shouted Suzi, as she and Buddy ran onto the playground, followed by Jessi pushing Marnie in her stroller.

Five more Kristy's Krushers T-shirts.

"We're here!" cried Karen as she and Andrew climbed out of their mother's car and their mom drove off. (This was not one of their weekends at our house.)

Andrew was wearing his Kristy's Krushers shirt.

Karen was wearing her shirt, too. It said Kristy's Crushers.

"Whoa, Karen!" I exclaimed. "How did that happen? Did your mom iron the letters on your shirts?"

Karen nodded.

"Well, she spelled our team name wrong on your shirt."

"*My* shirt is spelled correctly," said Karen. "It'll be the only one, too. Crushers. C-R-U-S-H-E-R-S. Crushers."

Karen sounded like she was in a spelling bee. I knew there was no changing her mind. She takes her spelling very seriously. Anyway, I didn't see why I should discourage that.

Kids kept pouring onto the playground. Soon all the Krushers had arrived, as well as some more onlookers. There were Jessi and Marnie, of course. And Mr. Perkins. He was sitting in the stands with Watson. Haley Braddock, Vanessa Pike, and Charlotte Johanssen (another kid our club sits for) had shown up, too. I guess just to watch the action. Plus, a couple of little boys I didn't recognize were hanging around.

I looked over at Jessi and she waved to me. She was giving Marnie Cheerios from a baggie. When you go places with a two-year-old, you have to bring along an awful lot of equipment — toys, munchies, baby wipes, extra clothes, you name it.

"Okay, Krushers!" I shouted. "Everybody over here! I've got news!"

Watson and I had decided that I should tell the kids about our game against the Bashers as soon as possible. Since I wasn't sure how some of them were going to react, I wanted to make the whole thing sound as exciting as possible. I called Haley over to sign for Matt.

"You guys look great!" I exclaimed when we were all sitting down.

"A real team, like I said before," added David Michael.

I'd never seen so many happy faces in one place.

"What's the news, Coach?" Jake Kuhn wanted to know.

"The news," I said, dragging the surprise out tantalizingly, "is that we . . . the Krushers . . . are going to play a *real* game . . . against another team."

A murmur ran through the crowd. If it was possible, the kids' faces lit up even more. (A good sign.)

"Who are we playing?" asked Jackie.

"A team called the Bashers."

"*Bart's* Bashers?" squeaked Max Delaney.

I couldn't tell whether he sounded excited or terrified.

"That's right."

"Are they good?" asked Jackie.

"I've never seen them play," I replied honestly, "but I know that they're a *little* older than you guys. I mean, just on the average, so — "

"But they're not Little Leaguers?" said Nicky Pike.

"Nope."

There was a moment of silence. Then Hannie Papadakis said, "This is going to be so, so cool." I think she got that from me.

And Matt Braddock raised his hand to attract my attention, then signed that he couldn't wait for the game and that the Bashers better get themselves ready for it.

"When is the game?" Haley asked me, signing for Matt at the same time.

"Two weeks from today," I answered, "so we better start working. We need to practice, and I also want to assign positions to some of you. We've got to have a really good pitcher, a really good shortshop, and really good basemen. We won't be switching around so much anymore. The pitcher is the most important position, though, and *everybody* will need to work on hitting, okay?"

"Okay!" yelled the kids.

"Are we ready to get to work?"

"Yes!"

"Are we going to work hard?"

"YES!"

"Are we going to beat the Bashers?"

"*YES!*"

And right at that moment, I got another one of my ideas. Cheerleaders! Boy, could we use them! And I bet the Bashers wouldn't have cheerleaders.

"Haley," I said. "I know you don't want to play ball, but how would you like to be a cheerleader? Maybe Vanessa could cheer, too. And Charlotte."

"Wow!" cried Haley. "Hey, Vanessa! Charlotte! Come here for a sec!"

The girls left the stands and ran to us. I told them my idea.

Vanessa was so excited she practically burst out of her skin, but Charlotte began to look guarded. "I don't know," she said. "All those people watching. . . ." Charlotte is really shy.

"Oh, please?" said Vanessa and Haley at the same time.

"Well, maybe I could help you make up some cheers and you guys could do them," said Charlotte slowly.

"That'd be great," I told her. I didn't want to force her into anything. Once, Claudia had kind of pressured her into being in a beauty pageant, and Charlotte had ended up running off the stage in tears.

"Two cheerleaders and one helper would be perfect," I told the girls. Charlotte is very smart, and I knew she'd write good cheers.

The girls grinned at each other excitedly.

"Boy!" exclaimed Myriah. "Cheerleaders and everything!"

"Yeah," said Jackie. "If we're going to have a real game with team T-shirts and cheerleaders, maybe we should sell refreshments."

"Mallory could help Nicky and Claire and me bake cookies," said Margo Pike.

"We could sell lemonade," suggested Suzi Barrett.

I thought for a moment. Refreshments sounded like a lot of fun — and a lot of work. "Who's going to sell the refreshments?" I asked. "We'll all be busy playing or cheering or coaching."

"Our brothers and sisters," said Max Delaney. "I bet Amanda would help."

I doubted that, but Charlie and Sam might help. The Pike triplets might, too. "Well, okay. But what are we going to do with the money we earn?" I asked. "Remember, it will be *team* money."

"Buy team hats," Jackie replied immediately.

"We really need them. Only some of us have hats, and they don't match."

So *that* was all settled.

"Great," I said. "But now we better do the most important thing of all — practice."

I got the kids all worked up again, then divided them into two sides for a game. They really needed to improve their teamwork.

"Nicky," I said, pulling Nicky Pike aside, "I think you're the best pitcher we've got, so from now on I want you and David Michael to pitch at all our practices. But *you'll* pitch in the game against the Bashers."

Nicky looked awed and proud.

The game got underway.

Vanessa and Haley stood on the sidelines shouting, "Bash those Bashers!" and stuff like that. Watson cheered loudly for Karen, Andrew, David Michael — and the rest of the team.

But not too long into the game, I caught Suzi Barrett turning somersaults in the outfield and Linny Papadakis, an imaginary microphone in his hand, pretending to be a sportscaster, when he was supposed to be playing shortstop. And Claire's batting average was still zero.

I shook my head.

Claire struck out and Jackie stepped up to

home plate. Nicky pitched the ball, Jackie swung the bat, and *CRACK!* He slammed the ball so hard that everyone knew he'd gotten a home run. Grinning, Jackie set off for first base. But before he reached it, we heard another sound.

CRASH!

The ball has gone right through a window of Stoneybrook Elementary. And not just any window, the window of the principal's office. Thank goodness it was a Saturday. No one would be —

A face appeared in the window. It was the principal's secretary. He was out the side door of the school in three seconds flat. (Maybe he'd want to play on our team.)

"Who threw that ball?" he shouted.

Poor Jackie stepped forward. "Me," he said. "I mean, I hit it. It was a home run," he added hopefully.

The man smiled. But he still told Jackie that the Rodowskys would have to pay for a new pane of glass.

When he went back inside, I announced that practice was over. The kids would never be able to concentrate now. I was sure of that.

Even so — despite the accident and sending the kids home early — Jessi told me later that

Buddy and Suzi were absolutely jubilant as they walked back to the Barretts' that afternoon. And Watson was so excited about the upcoming game that he made David Michael, Andrew, and Karen excited, too.

T-shirts, cheerleaders, refreshments, a real game coming up. It had been one of the biggest days in Krusher history.

CHAPTER 10

Tuesday

Whoa! Something is going on.
And Kristy, it has to do with you
and that other team, the Blasters
or whoever they are. It doesn't
really have anything to do with
baby-sitting, except that I saw
this incident while I was sitting.
See, Mrs. Perkins and Mrs. Newton
asked me to take Myriah, Gabbie
and Jamie to the Tuesday Krushers
practice. I was in the stands
watching the game when the
Blasters came by, and Kristy, you
kind of got mad at their coach.
But before you got mad, you got,
oh... I better stop before I get
myself in trouble. Just one more
thing. The Perkins girls and Jamie

were upset when we walked home this afternoon. They were really annoyed with what the Blasters did, and embarrassed about it, too, I think....

T alk about *Whoa!* Dawn doesn't miss a thing. Her notebook entry was pretty meaty, if you know what I mean. The only thing she got wrong was the Blasters. She meant the Bashers, of course. I wished she hadn't noticed quite so much about me and Bart. And I *really* wished she hadn't written about us in the notebook. I'd have to talk to her about that.

The thing is, I hadn't mentioned Bart to any of my friends, even Mary Anne. I mean, I haven't mentioned how I feel about him. The club members know that the Krushers are playing a rival team soon, and some of them know that the coach of that team is named Bart, but none of them knows about my Gigantic Crush on him. Usually, that's the sort of thing us club members share, but for some reason, I wanted to keep Bart private. And after what happened at the practice, I was glad I'd been doing just that.

The practice got off to a pretty normal start.

The kids arrived on time (Dawn got her kids to the playground early — she is *so* organized), and they were all wearing their T-shirts again. It was a much warmer day, so they didn't have to wear them over other clothes. I looked at my team. Smiling faces, new Kristy's Krushers T-shirts, running shoes with the laces tied or the Velcro straps fastened, neat blue jeans — all twenty kids. . . . No, nineteen of them. Nineteen tidy team members and one mess, our walking disaster. Jackie's jeans were muddy, his shoes were untied, and his shirt was on backward and already had a hole in it. Even his hair was a mess. Oh, well.

"All right, Krushers!" I called.

To my surprise, I heard a shout: "Krush those Bashers! Crash those Bashers! Bash those Bashers out of sight!"

Our cheerleaders were on hand.

Then I heard another sound. It was a laugh. I turned away from my team members, who were lined up, ready to count off by twos, and saw — Bart and about ten of his Bashers. Bart was sitting in the stands, gazing intently at our team, but his Bashers were hanging around behind the catcher's cage. I guessed they were his Bashers, anyway. They were sturdy-looking boys wearing matching red baseball caps. But Bart wasn't paying much attention to them.

"Bart!" I cried. I'm sure I blushed. My knees turned to water, but I managed to run over to him. "What are you doing here?" I asked.

"Just checking up on our competition," he replied coolly. "That's legal."

"Oh." I said. I felt something like a rock settle in the pit of my stomach. "We — we haven't checked you guys out."

"Come on and check us out then. It's a free country."

Bart tried to smile, but I frowned. This didn't seem like the boy I'd talked to under the streetlight. Was this a side of him I didn't know yet? Or was he only like this on the ball field? (Like Claire and her baseball tantrums?) I mean, I would do anything for my Krushers. Maybe Bart felt the same way about his Bashers.

I didn't know what to say to Bart, so I just walked back to my team. I felt crushed. (Krushed.)

As I passed the Bashers I heard a few snickers from them. And some whispered comments which I know Bart couldn't hear.

"Look at that messy kid. He looks like Pig-Pen from Peanuts!" (Jackie.)

"Look at that baby-baby with the wiffle ball! I don't believe it — a *wiffle* ball!" (That was Gabbie, her T-shirt covering her round two-

and-a-half-year-old tummy. The only ball I'd allow her to hit was a wiffle ball. And in order to throw it, the pitcher had to stand about five feet away from her. How would I handle that in the game against the Bashers? I hadn't even thought about that, but I was determined to put every one of my kids in the game, even Gabbie and Claire, and even if it was only for a few minutes. Watson and I had decided that was important.)

More comments:

"Look at fatso!" (Okay, so Jake Kuhn was a little overweight.)

"But *that* kid looks like a good pitcher." (Nicky. I was relieved to see that the Bashers appeared worried.)

In the stands, Dawn was watching us. She was taking everything in. She'd seen me have my talk with Bart, and she'd seen Bart's kids snicker at the Krushers. She'd figured out that they were Bashers (or Blasters), and she was surprised. She was surprised because she knew Bart's team was from my neighborhood, which is pretty far away. The Blasters must be awfully curious, thought Dawn, to come all the way across town just to watch a Krushers practice. Either that, or they were nervous.

I decided to ignore Bart and his stupid Bashers. I pretended they weren't even there.

At least I tried to. It wasn't easy. I could almost feel Bart's eyes on me.

"Okay, Krushers!" I shouted. "Practice game! Practice game! Count off by twos! Let's get rolling!"

The Krushers divided up. David Michael and Nicky were the pitchers, and Nicky's side was at bat first.

David Michael pitched to Margo Pike. She hit a pop fly. One out.

It's too bad I have such good hearing because I heard one of the Bashers say, "What can you expect from a *girl?*"

From a girl? Weren't there any girl Bashers? Even though I had decided to ignore our audience, I turned around to look at Bart. He was still sitting in the stands, watching the game.

Myriah Perkins was up next. She hit the ball and ran to second base. She really should only have made it to first, but Jackie was in the outfield and had so much trouble getting hold of the ball, you'd have thought there was margarine on his hands.

I heard a couple of hoots from behind me. "Pig-Pen sure can't catch," somebody shouted.

I whirled around to see Bart's reaction to his Basher's behavior, but two of the other Bashers were talking to him. For just a moment, I wondered if they were actually distracting him so he *couldn't* hear. . . . Nah.

Matt Braddock was up next. Good, I thought. Now we'll show those Bashers our stuff. If only Jackie weren't in the outfield. . . .

Matt got two strikes, but whacked the ball hard on the third try. He let out an animal-sounding yell, which he sometimes does when he's excited (of course, he has no idea how he sounds), and he took off. When he reached second base, he paused, seeing that Myriah had stopped at third. She signed to Matt to stay put.

At that, the laughter behind me was so loud that the only thing I could be glad of was that Matt wasn't able to hear it. The Krushers looked over at the Bashers. I could see the same thing registering on all their faces at the same time: They knew their competition was watching, and they knew they ought to start playing well.

But just then, one kid said loudly, "A dummy! They've even got a dummy on their team!"

Bart, why don't you make your kids shut up? I wondered. But I could see that one of his players had asked him for pitching tips, which Bart was giving out grudgingly. (He wanted to watch our team.) Now why would a kid need pitching tips in the middle of a scouting-out-the-other-team venture? Bart's Bashers *were* distracting him. I felt very angry. Why wasn't Bart picking up on what his team was doing?

Haley charged over to the Basher who had just insulted her brother. She stood inside the catcher's cage, nose-to-nose with the boy on the other side of the wire fence.

"That 'dummy,' " she said with clenched teeth, "is my brother, and if you call him a dummy one more time, I will personally rearrange your face."

The kid just stared at Haley, but she stared back until she had stared him down.

The Bashers grew silent. They watched Haley walk back to Vanessa and Charlotte, where the three girls held a hurried conference. Then Charlotte returned to the stands, and Vanessa and Haley began jumping around, shouting, "Krushers crush, Bashers bash, but we'll get you Bashers in a flash!"

After Haley's outburst, the Bashers were quiet for two whole innings. They were still hanging around the catcher's cage (actually, four of them were hanging *on* it, several feet off the ground), but they were quiet. They were quiet until Jackie, running home, somehow couldn't stop in time and ran right into the catcher's cage.

Two of the Bashers were knocked to the ground, like flies flicked off a screen door.

"Way to go, Pig-Pen!" yelled one Basher, and I shot a killer look at Bart, but he was now bending over, trying to unknot his sneakers, which I could see had been tied together, undoubtedly by his stupid Bashers.

If Bart couldn't control his team, I thought, then he really shouldn't be coaching.

Jackie looked at me with tear-filled eyes, and I couldn't blame him. I called an end to the practice.

Dawn told me later that as she walked Myriah, Gabbie, and Jamie home that afternoon, Jamie sulked, Gabbie cried, and Myriah held her sister's hand protectively.

"Those boys were mean," Gabbie commented, and then hiccupped.

"They were," Myriah agreed, "but we won't be mean back, will we? . . . Will we?" she said again when no one answered her.

"No," agreed Gabbie and Jamie at last.

And I knew that was true. My Krushers would not be mean.

CHAPTER 11

I couldn't believe it! How did it get to be Friday already?

It was the day before the Krushers' game against the Bashers. We were holding a special final practice. Us Baby-sitters Club members were even giving up our meeting so we could cheer the Krushers on.

The day was very important. It was my last chance to work with the Krushers. I knew the practice might be a tough one, though. The kids were pretty wound up. But they needed to practice if they wanted to win — and they all wanted to win.

I wanted them to win, too. Not just because I'm competitive, but because I wanted Kristy's Krushers to know what it felt like to be winners — instead of kids who were afraid to be part of Little League, who were afraid of Bart's Bashers, who had zero batting averages, who were called "Pig-Pen" and "dummy," and who broke windows and ran into catcher's cages.

And by the end of our practice, I truly thought the Krushers had a shot at winning, even though I had never seen the Bashers play. I hadn't done what Bart had done — check out the competition. I was scared to. I was also scared to admit that, even to myself. So I tried not to think about it.

At most of our practices, a few people would be sitting in the stands watching: club members who had brought kids over to play, maybe a couple of interested parents or a brother or sister, and the cheerleaders. But that Friday, twenty people were in the stands!

The Krushers were awed.

I was awed.

Jessi, Mal, Claud, Dawn, and Mary Anne were there, of course. So were Mrs. Newton and Lucy, Mrs. Perkins and Laura, Watson (taking the afternoon off from work), the triplets, and a few other people. There was no sign of the Bashers, and I breathed a sigh of relief.

Then, just as I was about to start our game, the cheerleaders showed up. Right away I noticed two things. One, they'd put together outfits for themselves — Kristy's Krushers T-shirts, matching flared blue-jean skirts, white knee socks, and sneakers. Two, Charlotte was wearing one of the outfits!

I ran over to the girls. "You look great!" I exclaimed. "The Krushers really appreciate your cheering. . . . And, Char, you're wearing an outfit, too. Does this mean you're going to cheer tomorrow? We'd really like that, but you don't have to, you know."

"I know," Charlotte replied, "and right now it just means I'm the head cheerleader because I made up all the cheers. But I *might* cheer tomorrow."

"She's thinking about it," Haley added.

Wow. I knew the Krushers meant a lot to their families and friends, but if they could inspire Charlotte to think about coming out of her shell, they must really be something. More and more, I was feeling that we just might, as Charlotte would say, bash those Bashers the next day!

I walked back to my team. I stood in front of them, ready to give them a pep talk, but for some reason I glanced into the stands first. My eyes met Watson's and he gave me the thumbs-up sign.

I grinned and gave him the sign back.

Then I faced my team. There they were — nineteen Krushers and Jackie. Oh, Jackie was a Krusher, too, all right. Don't get me wrong.

It's just that he, well, he *did* look a little like Pig-Pen. He was still the only kid with a hole in his T-shirt. He was the only kid whose shoes were untied. Even the littlest kids were neat and tidy. Jackie was our walking disaster. Although he *had* been playing better lately. His hitting had really improved. It was just that he had so many accidents.

"Okay, Krushers," I began, "you all know what tomorrow is."

"A game," replied Jackie.

"Well, our *big* game," I said. "Against the . . ."

"Bashers!" shouted the Krushers.

"And what are we going to do?" I cried.

"Beat them!"

"What?"

"Beat them!"

"Louder!"

"BEAT THEM!"

"And how are we going to do that?" I asked. Silence.

"By playing our . . ." I prompted my team.

"Best!"

"Right. That's all I can ask of you," I told the Krushers. "That's all you can ask of yourselves."

This was something Watson had told me many times. In fact, it was something he had told Karen and Andrew and my brothers and me many times, and not just about playing ball. About anything. Once, I was giving him the news that I'd gotten a C+ on a math test. Now, a C+ is not a bad grade, but I usually get mostly A's and a few B's. Watson looked thoughtful and asked, "Did you study for this test? Did you do your best?"

"Yes," I answered. "Honest. It's just that we're doing pre-algebra now and it's really hard."

"Your best is all you can expect," said Watson. "If you want, I'll give you some extra help, but since you did your best, I'm not disappointed. I'm proud of you."

"I *would* like some help," I'd told him.

Now, standing before the Krushers, I said to them again, "Just do your best." And without even looking into the stands, I knew that Watson was smiling at me.

I divided the Krushers into teams, and our last practice game got underway. Gabbie was up at bat first, so David Michael, who was pitching, had to move in pretty close to her. He tossed the wiffle ball. Gabbie missed. He tossed it again. Gabbie missed. He tossed it a third time, and Gabbie swung and hit it. She ran as fast as she could go (which wasn't nearly as fast as the rest of the kids), and she reached first base.

"Stop! Stop!" I cried. (Sometimes Gabbie would just keep running.)

Jackie was up next and hit the ball (a regular one) right away. He ran to first while Gabbie made it to second. (Everyone tried to ignore the fact that Jackie had tripped over the bat as he tossed it away.)

Third up was — Oh, no, it was Claire.

She struck out. But she did not throw a tantrum.

Fourth up was Andrew. Well, this could be interesting, I thought. Andrew sort of bunted the ball. He ran to first, Jackie ran to second, and Gabbie safely reached third.

The bases were loaded. "Bases are loaded!" I called.

Buddy Barrett was at bat next and, to everyone's surprise, but especially his own, he struck out. Two outs.

Karen's turn.

"Two outs and the bases are loaded!" I announced.

Nothing like pressure.

"Go, Karen!" yelled Watson from the stands.

Karen concentrated. She stuck her tongue between her teeth, kept her eye on the ball —

and hit a home run! The ball sailed into the school parking lot. Four runs batted in!

The rest of the game went just like that. It was exciting. The Krushers played well and hard. The final score was 13-12. I was so pleased I was ready to explode. And the cheerleaders screamed so loudly I had to tell them to calm down. I didn't want them to be hoarse the next day.

At the end of the game, everyone in the stands rushed onto the field. Watson slapped high and low fives with Karen, Andrew, and David Michael. Then he gave me a hug. "You are doing a terrific job, Kristy," he said seriously. "You've really changed these kids. All of them."

"We'll see tomorrow," I replied.

"No," said Watson, "you've already done it. Tomorrow hardly matters — I mean, in the greater scheme of things." I knew what Watson meant, even if he did sound a little jerky right then.

"Well, come on, kids. I'll drive you home," said Watson.

I was about to walk off with him and Karen and my brothers when someone tapped me on the shoulder.

I turned around.

"Bart!" I exclaimed, feeling more surprised than excited. When had he arrived? "How long have you been here?" I asked.

"Long enough," he replied. I supposed he meant, "Long enough to see how good the Krushers have gotten."

"Want to walk home?" he asked.

"Okay," I said, even though it would be a long walk and I was tired. "Watson, I guess I'm walking," I told him. "I'll see you later."

I was curious to see why Bart wanted to walk me home and what he had to say, but that head-over-heels feeling was gone. I felt as if I didn't quite trust him. He had hurt me.

Bart and I left the playground, and I just knew the members of the Baby-sitters Club were staring at me. Their mouths were probably hanging open, and I bet their eyes were bugging out. I'm sure they thought that Bart and I were interested in each other. I wish *I* could have been so sure of what was going on.

"You guys are getting good," Bart told me when we reached the street and had a little more privacy.

A-*ha!*

"Thanks," I said. I was about to add something about how hard each of the players had worked, but I didn't want to give anything away to Bart. After all, he was the Bashers' coach.

He was the enemy.

So all I said was, "Tomorrow, I'll want to put Gabbie — you know, the little one? — in the game for awhile. She has to hit a wiffle ball. So your pitcher will have to move in closer. Is that okay?"

"Sure," replied Bart, stuffing his hands in his pockets. I think he started to say something else then, like I had done a few moments earlier, but he closed his mouth.

After that, neither one of us knew what to say. So we just walked along silently. When we reached my house, Bart said, " 'Bye, Kristy," and I replied. " 'Bye." Then he added, "Good luck tomorrow," and I said, "You too."

I walked inside feeling confused and disappointed.

CHAPTER 12

"Kristy! Kristy! Hey, Coach! Get up! It's game day!"

Karen was standing about two inches away from me. It was the next morning, and she was trying to wake me up. She had already raised my shades and turned on my radio.

"Coach!" she called again. You'd have thought it was Christmas morning.

"Okay," I mumbled. "I'm getting up."

"Really?"

"Honest. But only if you'll leave me a — only if you'll go downstairs and eat a good breakfast. Tell Andrew and David Michael to do the same thing. You guys need plenty of energy today."

"Okay!" Karen bounced out of my room. She already had enough energy for her whole team, and the Bashers, too.

I sat up. I looked out the window. The day

107

was sunny, the sky was cloudless. Maybe that was a good omen. Of course, the weather was just the same over at Bart's house. He was probably thinking it was a good omen for the Bashers. So then, what kind of omen was it? (That's why omens are stupid.)

I put on my coaching outfit — my Krushers T-shirt, blue jeans, sneakers, and my baseball cap with the collie dog on it. Jackie was right. We needed team hats.

Then I ran downstairs. I found Karen, Andrew, and David Michael at the breakfast table, along with Charlie. The three Krushers were already dressed for the game.

"Good work," I said to Karen. "I'm glad you guys are eating — "

I stopped. I looked at their breakfasts. Cheerios, toast, scrambled eggs, fruit, bacon, and fried potatoes. Andrew had a milk mustache, and Karen and David Michael were drinking glasses of orange juice in addition to everything else.

"Karen," I said, "I know I told you to eat a good breakfast, but you don't want to make yourselves sick." I had never seen so much food.

"We're bulking up, Coach," David Michael told me.

"What do you know about bulking up?" I

asked. Then I looked at Charlie, who had suddenly made himself very busy at the stove. "Charlie?" I said.

"I didn't know they'd take me seriously," he explained.

"Well, just eat as much as you want," I told the Krushers. "Don't force it. Charlie will eat anything that's left over, since he's the human Hoover."

I buttered a piece of toast. I ate it slowly. I glanced at my watch. "Nine-thirty!" I cried. "Oh, my gosh! I better get going! I have a lot to do! Where are Mom and Watson? Where's Sam? Did he bake those brownies? Where are the tables for the refreshments?"

"Kristy! Kristy!" Watson was entering the kitchen. "Calm down, honey," he said. "Your mom ran to the store for a few minutes and Sam's on his way downstairs. Everything is under control."

"Are the brownies finished?"

"Yes."

"Did someone find those tables in the basement."

"Yes."

"Did the — "

Ring, ring.

"I'll get it!" I shrieked. I dashed for the phone, but Charlie reached it first, that rat.

"Hello?" he said. Then, "For you, Kristy."

I could have told him that.

I took the phone from him. "Hello?"

"Hey, Coach. This is Jake," said Jake Kuhn.

"Hi. What's up?"

"My mom says I have to wash my T-shirt before the game today. Is that true?"

"Well, *I* didn't say you have to wash your shirt, but if your shirt is dirty, then you should probably — "

"Mo-om!" Jake interrupted me, turning away from the phone. "Coach says she didn't say I have to wash my shirt."

"Jake! Jake!" I cried. Oh, brother, the last thing I needed was a parent mad at me.

"What?" said Jake.

"Wash your shirt," I told him.

No sooner had I hung up than the phone rang again. Since my hand was still on the receiver, there was no way Charlie could answer it first.

"Hello?" I said, praying it wasn't Jake calling back.

"Is this Kristy Thomas, the coach of the Krushers?" asked a small voice.

"Yes. Who's this?"

"Suzi Barrett."

"Hi, Suzi!" I exclaimed, but I was wondering, *Now* what?

110

"Buddy was saying," Suzi began, "that when you're playing a *real* game against *another team*, you're allowed to have four strikes before you're out."

"Buddy's teasing you," I told Suzi. "The rules are the same in any game."

"Okay. 'Bye."

Suzi hung up.

Mom walked in the back door then, and I nearly got hysterical over the refreshment-stand business, which I was beginning to be sorry I'd agreed to. Why can't I be cool-headed like Mallory, or calm in an emergency like Mary Anne, or as organized as Dawn?

"Mom!" I burst out, before she had even put the grocery bag on the counter. "I realized we should have paper towels or napkins or something at the refreshment stand — "

Mom pulled an economy-size pack of napkins out of her bag.

"And I forgot to remind you to buy paper cups for the lemon — "

Mom pulled out several packages of cups. Then she crossed the kitchen to me and took my face in her hands. "Don't worry, sweetie," she said. "The refreshment stand is taken care of. Sam and Charlie will run it. If everyone brings the food they promised to prepare, we'll be in good shape. All *you* need to worry about is your team." She glanced at the breakfast table.

David Michael, Andrew, and Karen were watching me nervously.

I smiled at them. "What are you going to do today, you guys?" I whispered.

"Beat the Bashers!" they shouted.

"Good," I said, and the phone rang again. "I'm sure it's for me," I told my mother as I reached for it.

It was. It was Jackie, the walking disaster, with a question about foul balls. He called five more times after that, with other softball questions, and each time he sounded more nervous. When the phone rang *again*, I picked it up and said, "Jackie, don't worry so much. I promise — "

"Kristy? This isn't Jackie."

"Mallory?"

"Yeah." She sounded kind of depressed.

"What's wrong? I know something's wrong."

"It's Nicky," she said. "He woke up this morning with a sore throat and swollen glands and a temperature of a hundred and one."

"Oh, no!" I cried. "That's terrible!"

"There's no way he can play today. Mom's taking him to the doctor."

"Okay," I replied slowly. "Thanks, Mal. Tell

Nicky I hope he's feeling better. I'll see you in a couple of hours."

When I hung up the phone that time, I left the kitchen. I went up to my bedroom to think. I was upset and I didn't want my Krushers to see that. After a few moments, though, I realized there was only one thing to do. I headed back downstairs and pulled David Michael into the laundry room for a conference.

"You," I told him, "and Jake Kuhn are going to pitch in the game today."

"Me?" he cried.

"Yup. Nicky's sick. You'll be the pitcher, Jake will be the relief pitcher. Do you think you can handle it?"

"I don't know. I'm a better pitcher than I used to be, but I'm still a klutz. And the Bashers call Jake 'Fatso.' It's hard to pitch when people are calling you names."

"Don't worry about Jake," I told him. "And just do your best. Okay?"

David Michael nodded. "Okay, Coach."

The rest of the morning sped by, and before I knew it, my family was loading things into our cars. There were so many people and so much stuff that we had to take two cars to the playground. We reached it an hour before the game was to begin.

Charlie and Sam set up the tables for the refreshments. Mom and Watson sat in the stands, out of our way. Funny, I almost wished Watson would tell me just one more time, "Do your best, Kristy."

But the Krushers began to arrive, so I had to take care of them. Some of them came with food to sell at the refreshment table. I sent them over to Charlie and Sam. Some of them had problems or worries. I tried to reassure them.

The stands were filling up. Since I didn't recognize a lot of the faces, I figured they must be Bashers supporters. But where were the Bashers themselves?

I gathered my team under a tree for a pep talk, and to explain our last-minute change in pitchers. "Jake," I said, "you'll be our relief pitcher, okay?"

"Okay," said Jake seriously.

"Now you guys go relax," I told the Krushers, "and Jackie?"

"Yeah?"

"You're looking good."

For once, the walking disaster looked more like a Krusher and less like Pig-Pen. His shoes were tied. His clothes were clean. The hole in his shirt had been mended. But his hair still stuck out in seventeen different directions.

"Hey, Coach," he said, tapping me on the arm, "look!"

The Bashers had arrived. They emerged from around a corner of the school and walked onto the playing field in a neat, straight line, led by Bart. Twenty-one boys. They were wearing Bashers T-shirts *and* matching red caps. They were followed by four girls in snazzy cheerleaders' uniforms.

I looked at my Krushers. Their faces fell.

What an entrance the Bashers had made.

CHAPTER 13

Before the game started, Bart and I held a conference. We talked about Gabbie and the wiffle ball again, and I reminded Bart that we would have to sign to Matt Braddock. Then we decided on a seven-inning game.

"If you want," Bart said, "I'll make an announcement about the innings. After that, we'll toss a coin to see who goes to bat first."

I nodded. Good. I may not be shy, but I didn't really want to make an announcement to all the people who were jamming the stands. And believe me, there were a lot of them. Plus, there was a crowd around the refreshment tables.

I looked everything over as I listened to Bart greet the fans. He said something like, "Welcome to the first official game between Bart's Bashers and Kristy's Krushers." (*First* official game?) Then he explained the rules of the day's game.

Almost everyone was listening. A few kids were clustered around the refreshment stand, though, and Charlie and Sam were busy making change. Our cheerleaders weren't paying any attention to Bart, either. They were scoping out the Bashers' cheerleaders, whom I'm sure they hadn't expected. *I* hadn't expected them. I bet Bart got the idea for cheerleaders when he was spying on our practice games.

The Krushers were scoping out the Bashers. If they were feeling at all the way they *looked*, it was not a good sign. My jumbled team of boys and girls, tiny kids and big kids (well, fatsos), and even a handicapped kid, a klutz, and a disaster, were facing a team of sturdy boys — no little kids, no fatsos or deaf kids or klutzes. I suddenly had the feeling that each Krusher was thinking, "We don't stand a chance."

I tried to send the Krushers a message with mental telepathy. *You do stand a chance, you do stand a chance.*

The game began. Bart was acting as umpire. The Krushers were at bat, and Max Delaney was up first. He seemed to be there forever, and finally, after ball four (and two strikes), he walked to first base.

Behind me, the Krushers were getting antsy. And out of the blue, who should appear to help me, but the rest of the Baby-sitters Club.

"I can't wait to play! I can't wait to play!" Karen cried. So Mary Anne gave her a piggyback ride around the refreshment stand.

Claudia played Simon Says with Gabbie, Myriah, and Jamie.

Dawn and Mal broke up an argument between Jake and Jackie.

And Jessi picked up and soothed a nervous Suzi Barrett.

They kept the Krushers calm and entertained while I kept my eye on the game.

Things weren't going too badly, although nothing exciting was happening. The next batter also walked to first while Max walked to second.

Ho-hum.

Then Jamie was at bat. I looked at the kid who was pitching to him. He was about ten, tall for his age, and had a good strong arm. He barreled the ball toward Jamie.

Jamie ducked.

The Bashers snickered.

That happened two more times.

"Three strikes, you're out!" shouted Bart.

Duh.

Claire was up next. Our cheerleaders caught sight of this and decided to give her a little boost.

"Krush those Bashers!" shouted Vanessa and Haley.

Claire struck out.

The Bashers' cheerleaders stepped forward. In a neat line, pom-poms flying, they belted out a cheer that I bet they hadn't written themselves. It was just too darn good.

Vanessa and Haley looked at each other. Then they looked at Charlotte, who shrugged. Then *every*one looked at Claire Pike. Why?

Because she was throwing a tantrum, that's why.

"Nofe-air! Nofe-air! Nofe-air!" she shrieked. Her face turned so red that her father had to step over a whole lot of people in the stands, run to Claire, take her aside, and calm her down.

From the stands came gentle laughter.

I let Mr. Pike handle Claire and looked at my team to see who was up next. It was time for a heavy hitter, and sure enough, Matt Braddock was up. I cringed, though, thinking of how the Bashers had laughed and called him a dummy before. They wouldn't dare do that in front of all the parents, would they?

No way! Not when Matt hit a home run! *Crack!* No signing was even needed. Matt just ran the bases, sending the two Krushers ahead of him home, too.

The score was 3-0, in favor of the Krushers.

"Outta sight! Outta sight! You hit that ball with all your might!" screamed Haley and Vanessa. They were jumping up and down enthusiastically, but somehow they didn't live up to the Bashers' cheering.

It didn't matter. When Matt reached home plate, the Krushers crowded around him, hugging him and signing to him. (Jessi told me one of the kids accidentally gave him the sign for "oven," but Matt didn't notice, and who cared anyway?) The excitement was uproarious. When it died down, Margo Pike stepped up to bat.

The Bashers must have had her pegged as an unreliable hitter, because immediately, their cheerleaders began chanting, "Strike out! Strike out!" which I thought was really mean.

Apparently, I wasn't the only one who thought so. The next thing I knew, the Pike triplets, dressed impressively in their Little League uniforms, joined Vanessa and Haley and began cheering with them. It was hard to understand what they were shouting, but they drowned out the Bashers' cheerleaders, and that was really all that mattered.

Unfortunately, it didn't help.

Margo struck out.

"Three outs!" yelled Bart unnecessarily, and

the Krushers gave up their bats and trotted onto the field. I'd thought they'd be devastated, but they looked fine. I even overheard Jackie say to David Michael, "*Three* runs. Can you believe it?"

They were proud!

The Krushers stationed themselves at their positions, while the Bashers were organized into their batting line-up. Once, while the kids were getting settled, my eyes met Bart's. We both looked away quickly.

Then I signalled to David Michael, who was already on the pitcher's mound.

He ran to me. "Yeah?" He looked nervous. But he also looked as if he were saying, with his eyes alone, "If you don't let me pitch, I'll kill you."

"David Michael," I said to him seriously, "just do your best."

His face broke into a big smile. "I will, Watson," he teased me.

I punched him on the arm and sent him back to the pitcher's mound, grinning.

David Michael's grin soon turned to gritted teeth. He simply was not as good as the Bashers' pitcher, and the Bashers kept getting runs. By the end of the inning, the score was Bashers 6, Krushers 3.

The teams changed sides again.

I started the second inning by putting Gabbie in the game for awhile. It was an easy time to do that, before things really got underway, and I ran out to the Bashers' pitcher with the wiffle ball and told him what was going on. I really should have told Bart, but I just couldn't face him.

The pitcher looked at the wiffle ball and rolled his eyes.

"She's only two and a half," I snapped, "so walk forward. Now."

The kid obeyed. And to give him credit, I have to say that he tossed the ball very nicely to Gabbie. He didn't try anything funny.

Gabbie hit the ball. The pitcher was so surprised that he fielded it badly, overthrew the base, and Gabbie was safe at first.

The walking disaster was up next and I caught sight of him near the refreshment stand, testing bats for their weight. He picked one up, swung it, put it down. Then he picked up another, swung it — and suddenly he must have had margarine on his hands again, because the bat slipped out of them and flew into the refreshment tables. *Very* luckily, it didn't hurt anyone. But the legs of both tables collapsed and the food began to slide every which way.

"Catch it! Catch it!" yelled Charlie. He and

Sam (and Jessi and Dawn, who happened to be standing nearby) dove frantically for the plates of brownies and cookies and cupcakes. They caught most things, but an entire cake went — *splat* — on a rock, and twelve cups of lemonade slid on top of it.

Absolutely everybody saw the accident. And everybody laughed.

I wanted to die, and I think Jackie felt the same way, but he marched up to bat instead. If he hadn't, he wouldn't have been able to live with himself. Besides, if he could hit a home run, then maybe everyone would forget about his disaster.

Jackie gripped the bat. He looked determined, but he must have been totally flustered. The first pitch was wild, but Jackie took a giant swing at it anyway, nearly losing his balance. (A few people in the stands couldn't help laughing.) The next pitch was right over home plate, and Jackie tried to get away with bunting it. He missed. Strike two. The third pitch was also well-placed. Jackie swung again — and his bat went flying. It nearly hit the pitcher, who gave Jackie a dirty look.

"Strike three, you're out!" shouted Bart.

Jackie was the picture of humiliation. You could see that his hopes of showing off had been completely dashed. His face started to crumple — and then he sort of stumbled. He sank to the ground, clutching his left ankle. "Oh!" he cried. "Oh, my ankle! I think I twisted it."

I ran to Jackie. His ankle looked fine to me (and I gave his parents the OK sign, so they wouldn't have to leave their places in the stands), but Jackie said it was killing him. "I better not play anymore," he added.

Jackie walked off the field, limping pitifully on his right ankle. . . . Wait a sec. His *right* ankle? No, now it was his left.

Aha! I thought. I knew exactly what Jackie was up to.

CHAPTER 14

I let Jackie sit on the sidelines until the first half of the second inning was over. Then I told Bart I needed time out. I didn't even really look at him. I just trotted by him, calling, "Time out!"

"Okay," Bart said to my back.

I sat down next to the walking disaster. I didn't waste any words. "Jackie," I said, "I'm putting you back in the game."

Jackie snapped to attention. "But — but I can't play, Coach!" he exclaimed. "I hurt my ankle." He began rubbing his right ankle.

"When you fell, you hurt your other ankle," I pointed out.

"Oops."

"Jackie, I know you're embarrassed. I also know you're a good player. You turned into one of our best hitters. And right now, we need you at first base. It's either you or Jamie

Newton, and you know what'll happen if a ball comes toward Jamie."

(Nothing like a little guilt.)

Jackie nodded. But all he said was, "Do I have to play?"

"No," I answered. "The only thing I ask of you Krushers is that you do your best. If you think this is your best, then okay. Personally, *I* think your best is over there at first base, not here on the sidelines. We really need you. We *want* you."

"You do?" said Jackie.

I nodded.

He sighed. "All right. I'll play."

Jackie stood up, and a few people in the stands clapped. (I think they were his parents and his brothers.) Then he ran onto the field.

Two of the Bashers laughed at him, and a third yelled, "Hit any good refreshment stands lately?" but Jackie ignored them.

David Michael (after losing his balance and tripping over absolutely nothing), pitched a fastball to the first Basher at bat. The Basher hit it, and Matt Braddock fielded it and sent it to Jackie, who caught it seconds before the kid touched base.

I took great pride in yelling, "Out!" even though I was not the umpire. But I made the mistake of glancing at Bart then, who looked at me murderously. I didn't care. Jackie was grinning like a jack-o'-lantern. His confidence had returned. And he, David Michael, Matt, and Myriah (who was our second basewoman) didn't let the Bashers get a single run during the rest of the inning.

The score was now 6-4. I don't think anyone was more surprised than the Bashers, even though they were ahead.

And no one was more surprised than *I* when our cheerleaders got to their feet and yelled, "Way to go! Way to go! The Krushers' score is sure to grow!" Why was I surprised? Because cheering along with the others was Charlotte — shy Charlotte Johanssen. I guess the Krushers' playing was just too much for her.

It was Charlotte's cheering, more than anything else, that suddenly gave me a surge of hope for my team. Maybe they could win after all.

The game continued. It was a warm day and the sun was beating down. The people in the stands put on sunglasses and took off jackets and sweaters. The frosting on the cupcakes and brownies at the refreshment stand began to melt. A few of the Bashers removed their hats because their heads were too hot, then put them back on because the sun was in their eyes.

I stuck a piece of gum in my mouth, chewed it, and followed the game.

In the third inning, Hannie Papadakis hit the ball — hard.

"Oh, my gosh!" she cried disbelievingly.

"Run, run!" I shouted to her.

"Oh, yeah!" she said, suddenly remembering — and managed to get around all the bases, beating the throw home. She even sent Margo home before her.

Two more runs for the Krushers.

The Bashers frowned. They gritted their teeth. They concentrated furiously on the game. When Gabbie was up next, I didn't even have to say anything to the pitcher. He just switched balls and moved forward.

At the end of the inning, the score was 8-6, still in favor of the Bashers.

At the end of the fourth inning, the Bashers were ahead 10-6, and Bart called for a "fourth-inning stretch." Everyone needed it — players, cheerleaders, fans, and coaches.

I wiped my forehead with the shoulder of my T-shirt (something Mom absolutely *hates* for me to do), and met up with the other members of the Baby-sitters Club.

"The Krushers are doing great!" cried Claudia.

"We're *losing*," I replied.

"But you're playing a very tough game," said Mary Anne, even though she knows next to nothing about sports. "Don't you see how the Bashers are acting now? You're giving them a run for their money."

"Yeah," agreed Mal. "I bet they thought they'd just walk onto the field, cream you, and leave. But your kids have gotten home runs and everything. Gabbie is amazing with that wiffle ball."

"Oh, but Jackie and the refreshment stand," I moaned.

"Everyone's forgotten about that," Dawn assured me. "He's played so well since then. Anyway, just look at him."

I looked. Jackie was by the stands, talking to his family. He was grinning, and he looked pretty pleased with himself.

As I watched Jackie, I noticed Karen signalling to me. Well, not exactly signalling; more like waving frantically. Karen just cannot be subtle.

"I better go see what she wants," I said.

I left my friends and trotted over to my family.

"Hi, Coach!" cried Karen. "I am so excited!"

"What a game!" Watson said.

"Yeah, we're winning," Andrew exclaimed.

"Wait a sec. No we're not," I had to tell him.

"Karen says we are."

"Karen, the Bashers are ahead of us. You know that," I said. "They've got ten runs and we've only got six."

"Only!" cried Karen. "Six is a lot. If we got six, we'll get more. I think we're going to beat the Bashers!"

I looked helplessly at Mom and Watson, but Mom shrugged and Watson said something about "hope springing eternal."

"What?" I said.

"The optimism of youth," Watson tried to explain.

I'd been about to ask him for some advice, but I decided not to. Not if he was in this dumb poetic mood.

"I better go check on Sam and Charlie," I said, and rushed off.

It was a good thing I did, too, because what with the fourth-inning stretch, they were overrun with lemonade requests. I snagged Mary Anne, and she and I helped them out. While we were filling cups, I overheard someone say, awed, "Those Krushers are really something."

I turned around. It was a Basher!

Ten minutes later, the game began again. An hour and fifteen minutes after that, it was just about over. It was the top of the seventh, the Bashers were still ahead, and the Krushers had two outs. Claire Pike went to bat.

Boy, I thought, trying to send her a mind message, if you've ever needed to hit that ball, it's right now.

Claire struck out.

The Bashers leaped to their feet and threw their hats in the air. The game was over.

The score was 16-11, and the Bashers had won. They had crushed the Krushers. I had seen it coming, of course. The Bashers had been ahead all along.

I guess I'd been hoping for a miracle.

I took off my collie hat and stuffed it in my back pocket. The Krushers were running off the field and the crowd was cheering. The cheerleaders were cheering, too — all of them, even Charlotte. And then I heard a third cheer: "Two, four, six, eight! Who do we appreciate? The Krushers! The Krushers! Yea!"

And an answering cheer: "Two, four, six, eight! Who do we appreciate? The Bashers! The Bashers! Yea!"

The Krushers and the Bashers were slapping five and pounding each other on the backs. The Krushers didn't look too disappointed, not even Karen.

"Hey, you Krushers!" I yelled.

My team separated from the Bashers and straggled over to me.

"Congratulations, you guys," I said. "You played a really good game. I mean it."

"Even though we lost?" Jackie ventured.

"Even though you lost. You were playing against kids who are older and bigger than most of you. And who have been a team longer than the Krushers have. And you got *eleven runs*. Do you know how terrific that is?"

"Yup," said Karen. "We do."

"And the next time we play the Bashers," said Jackie, "maybe we'll beat them."

I grinned. "Okay, you guys. Time to go home. Find your parents or your brothers and sisters. Andrew, Karen, and David Michael, let's go help Sam and Charlie."

People began to drift away from the playground. Mary Anne left with Logan. Jessi walked off with Mallory and the Pikes. But Claudia and Dawn stayed and counted the money Sam and Charlie had taken in at the refreshment stand.

"Wow!" said Dawn a few minutes later when the counting was done. "This ought to buy hats for your team."

"I'll say," I agreed. "Thanks, Sam. Thanks, Charlie. The Krushers really appreciate your help."

"No problem," said Charlie, as he folded up the tables.

I checked to make sure that there were no stray cups or napkins on the ground, and then I turned to walk toward Mom's station wagon.

"Hey, Kristy!" called a voice.

I would know that voice anywhere. It was Bart's.

CHAPTER 15

Even though Bart was calling me, I didn't turn around right away. I stalled just long enough to see all sorts of things happen — Sam and Charlie nudge each other, Dawn and Claudia raise their eyebrows at each other, and Mom and Watson wink at each other.

Oh, brother. Did they all know there was something more (maybe) between Bart and me than just coaching our teams?

"Yeah?" I said, turning around.

Guess what? Bart wanted the two of us to walk home together again. So we did.

"See you later," I said to my family. Then, " 'Bye!" I called to Claud and Dawn. "I'll phone you tonight."

"You better," Claud replied mischievously, glancing at Bart. "If you don't, I'll call you."

Bart and I walked off sort of quickly. As soon as we left the playground, Bart said, "Well, congratulations!"

"On what?" I replied.

"On the Krushers' game, what else?"

"Oh, that," I said.

"They were great!"

"Some of them."

"*All* of them."

"Jamie Newton still ducks balls, and Claire Pike still has a zero batting average and throws tantrums."

"Maybe. But I noticed something today. Your team has total dedication."

"What do you mean?" I asked.

"I mean that they would do anything for the team or anyone on it. They may not be excellent players, but being part of a team means a *lot* to them. I could see it in their faces. I saw it every time one of them was at bat, especially kids like Jamie and Claire. I could almost hear them saying to themselves, 'This time I'm going to get that ball. I'm going to do it for my team. I know I've never done it before, but I'm going to do it now.' I think your kids realize that they couldn't be on any other team — at least not easily — so they're, like, really fierce about the Krushers."

Bart paused. Then he added, "That's why I got so nervous about them."

"You got nervous about the Krushers?" I said.

"Sure. I'll admit that I brought my kids by that day just to show them they really didn't have to worry about the game — that your kids were no threat. But when I saw them play, I got nervous. I could tell they were really going to hang in during the game."

"Wow," I said. Maybe I'd been too hard on myself — and on the Krushers. Or maybe I'd just set my expectations in the wrong places. What was so important about winning?

"Anyway, what's so important about winning?" I said to Bart.

"Yeah. . . ." he answered uncertainly.

Then we laughed.

"I guess we both like to win," I said.

"I'm pretty competitive," Bart admitted. "My parents say I'm *too* competitive."

"And I like to be in charge, running things," I told him.

"Well, you can do that when you coach."

"I know. But when I'm in charge of something, I like for it to work out, too. I like to win, just like you. . . . My friends and I have this club, the Baby-sitters Club. It's really a business. It was my idea, I'm the president, and the club is a big success. We get tons of jobs. If it weren't a success, though, I don't know what I'd do."

"Would you quit?"

I shrugged.

"Are you going to quit coaching the Krushers? I mean, since you lost today?"

I thought for a moment — just a moment. "No way!" I cried.

"Then winning probably isn't as important to you as you think it is," said Bart.

"You sound like a psychiatrist or something," I said, laughing.

Bart and I stepped off the curb to cross a street, and a car came zooming around a curve.

"Kristy, look out!" Bart grabbed my hand and pulled me back to the sidewalk. We were safe — but Bart didn't let go of my hand, even though he certainly could have. Instead, he held onto it until we had crossed the street.

"Nice hat," Bart commented a few minutes later. (I was wearing my baseball cap again.) "What's with the collie?"

"Oh, it's my favorite kind of dog. I wear this in remembrance of Louie. He was our collie. We had to have him put to sleep. We got Shannon after Louie died."

"Put to sleep," Bart repeated. "Wow. If we ever had to do that to Twinkle . . ." Bart's voiced trailed away. Then, "Kristy?"

"Yeah?"

"Remember when Jackie — is that his name? — ran into the catcher's cage that time?

Well, I apologize for what the Bashers said to him. I apologize for what they said to all your kids. I found out later that they'd been mean, but I was getting too worried about the Krushers to notice it at the time. All I could think about was our game."

"That's okay," I replied. "Maybe your kids gave my kids a little backbone. Besides, Jackie *is* a walking disaster. I can't tell whether he's just accident-prone, or if he lives in another time zone or something."

Bart laughed.

After that, I guess neither one of us could think of anything to say, because we were pretty quiet for awhile. I felt embarrassed and began casting around in my mind, trying to dredge up *some* subject to talk about with Bart. But what? My family? My school? Or I could ask him a question. I could say, "So, do you have any pets besides Twinkle?" or "What's your school like?" or "Do you have any brothers or sisters?" "Do you like me?"

I had just settled on the school question, which seemed like a safe one, when Bart said, sounding very nervous, "Um, Kristy, I have a question to ask you."

"Okay," I replied. Was Bart going to ask if *I* liked *him?*

"I was wondering. . . . I mean, I know the

last couple of weeks have been sort of difficult for us, but now we've both admitted that we're competitive, and we have one game behind us and we survived it. . . ." (What was Bart leading up to?) "So . . . how about another game between the Krushers and the Bashers? Say, in two weeks?"

"Okay," I replied, feeling a little let down.

"Wait," Bart went on. "Only on one condition."

"On one condition?"

"Yes. That in between games we act like something other than rival coaches."

"What do you mean?"

"Well, how about like friends? Or . . . maybe we could go out sometime. To a ball game or something. Would that be okay with you?"

I didn't pause for even a split second. "Sure!"

"Good," Bart replied. We both smiled.

We had reached our neighborhood, and pretty soon Bart would leave me at the end of my driveway. I wished our walk home didn't have to end, even though I was dead tired — but probably not as tired as the Krushers. I'd seen Gabbie nearly asleep in her father's arms as the Perkinses left the playground. And Andrew had looked ready for a nap.

"Well?" said Bart.

There we were, at my driveway.

"Well . . . I guess I'll be seeing you soon," I said.

"Before the game," replied Bart firmly.

"Great! Maybe you'd like to meet my friends sometime. I think you'd like them."

"Okay. . . . Can I come to a meeting of the Baby-sitters Club?"

"Do you want to be a baby-sitter?"

"No."

"Then I'll introduce you some other time. Meetings are serious."

"Deal," Bart said. Then he grinned. "See ya . . . Coach!" He turned and started home.

I watched Bart walk away. Then I turned around. I saw Watson gardening in the front flower bed and I ran to him.

"Hi!" I called.

Watson looked up from his work. "Hi, there. We didn't get to talk after the game. But I wanted to tell you that it was terrific, of course. I knew it would be, win or lose."

"You did? How'd you know that?" I stood at the edge of the garden and watched Watson turn peat moss into the soil.

"Because you were the Krushers' coach. That's how I knew." Watson straightened up. The gardens are his domain. He's totally happy when he's gardening.

"Thanks, Watson," I said. If he hadn't been

covered with peat moss, I think I would have hugged him. Instead I blurted out, "Bart wants me to go to a ball game with him. He wants us to be friends." Or maybe more than friends, I thought. But it was a pretty scary thought. Was I ready to be more than just friends with a boy?

"Wonderful," said Watson, smiling.

"I better go inside," I said. "I have a few calls to make."

I ran into our house. Suddenly, I was bursting with excitement and energy. I found Mom and told her all about Bart. Then I called Mary Anne, Dawn, and Claudia and told each of them about Bart.

Then I made a fourth phone call. "Hello?" I said. "Is Jackie there?"

"This is Jackie."

"Hi, it's Kristy Thomas. I just wanted to tell you how proud I am of you. You played well today. And you were very brave to go back in the game after your, um, accident."

"Wow! Thanks, Coach. You called just to tell m — Oops!"

CRASH!

"What was that?" I asked.

"A lamp," replied the walking disaster. "I just broke a lamp."

Some things never change.

About the Author

ANN M. MARTIN did *a lot* of baby-sitting when she was growing up in Princeton, New Jersey. Now her favorite baby-sitting charge is her cat, Mouse, who lives with her in her Manhattan apartment.

Ann Martin's Apple Paperbacks are *Bummer Summer, Inside Out, Stage Fright, Me and Katie (the Pest)*, and all the other books in the Baby-sitters Club series.

She is a former editor of books for children, and was graduated from Smith College. She likes ice cream, the beach, and *I Love Lucy*; and she hates to cook.

Look for #21

MALLORY AND THE TROUBLE WITH TWINS

"Can we see what's in the Kid-Kit?" asked one of the twins as Mrs. Arnold started her car in the garage.

(A quick glance at the bracelet.) "Sure, Marilyn," I replied, and Marilyn beamed. The twins must really love Kid-Kits. I'd have to remember to bring mine with me each time I sat.

"I like to read," said Marilyn.

"Let's see, then. Here's *Baby Island*. And here's *Charlie and the Great Glass Elevator*. Oh, here are three of the Paddington books."

"Paddington!" exclaimed both twins.

"We love him!" said Carolyn.

In a flash, Carolyn had chosen *Paddington Marches On*, Marilyn had chosen *Paddington Abroad*, and each twin was lying on her bed with her legs crossed, reading happily.

"You guys are so cute!" I couldn't help exclaiming. "Look at you. I wish I had my camera. You look like bookends."

The twins exchanged a troubled glance.

"Boggle," Marilyn whispered across the room to Carolyn. (Or did Carolyn whisper to Marilyn? I couldn't read their bracelets.)

Carolyn nodded. Then the twins went back to their books.

But not for long.

"Oom-bah," said Carolyn a few minutes later, and the girls tossed the books aside and got to their feet.

With another sidelong glance at each other, they did the last thing I'd expected them to do. Very slowly, they removed their bracelets. They tossed them onto their beds. Then they ran around the room, jumping back and forth, darting from side to side.

"Hey, you guys!" I cried. "What are you doing?"

"Chad. Pom dover glop," said one.

"Huh?"

"*Now* tell us apart," said Marilyn-or-Carolyn.

"I can't," I replied helplessly. "You don't have your bracelets on."

"Do you like to baby-sit?"

"Sure."

"Well, you won't like to sit for *us*."

Here's some news about other books in The Baby-sitters Club series by Ann M. Martin

#1 *Kristy's Great Idea*

Kristy thinks the Baby-sitters Club is a great idea. She and her friends Claudia, Stacey, and Mary Anne all love taking care of kids. But nobody counted on crank calls, wild pets, and uncontrollable two-year-olds! Having a Baby-sitters Club isn't easy, but Kristy and her friends won't give up till they get it right!

#2 *Claudia and the Phantom Phone Calls*

Claudia has been getting some mysterious phone calls when she's out baby-sitting. Could they be from the Phantom Jewel Thief who's operating in the area? Claudia has always liked *reading* mysteries, but she doesn't like it when they *happen* to her!

#3 *The Truth About Stacey*

The truth about Stacey is her parents want to find a miracle cure for her diabetes. They're making Stacey's life so hard! The other Baby-sitters are busy fighting the Baby-sitters Agency. How can they help Stacey and save the club, too?

#4 Mary Anne Saves the Day

Mary Anne's never been a leader of the Baby-sitters Club. Now there's a big fight among the four friends. It's bad enough when Mary Anne has to eat at the lunch table all alone. But when she has to baby-sit a sick child with no help from her friends — it's time to take charge!

#5 Dawn and the Impossible Three

Poor Dawn! It's not easy being the newest member of the Baby-sitters Club. She's got three impossible kids to take care of. And Kristy thinks things were better *without* Dawn around. It'll take a lot of work to make things run smoothly again, but Dawn's up to the challenge!

#6 Kristy's Big Day

It's a big day for Kristy, all right — she's a bridesmaid in her mother's wedding! And if that's not enough, she and the other Baby-sitters Club members have *fourteen* wedding-guest kids to take care of. Only the Baby-sitters Club could cope with this one!

#7 Claudia and Mean Janine

This summer the Baby-sitters Club is starting a play group in the neighborhood. Claudia can't wait for it to begin — it'll give her some time away from her mean big sister. But then her grandmother has a stroke . . . and the whole summer changes.

#8 Boy-Crazy Stacey

Who needs baby-sitting when there are boys around? Stacey and Mary Anne are mother's helpers at the Jersey shore, and Stacey's mind is on hunky lifeguard Scott. Mary Anne's doing the work of two baby-sitters . . . but how can she tell Stacey that Scott's too old, without breaking Stacey's heart?

#9 The Ghost at Dawn's House

Creaking stairs, noises behind the wall, a secret passage — there must be a ghost at Dawn's house! The Baby-sitters find themselves and one of their charges wrapped up in a mystery. Will they be able to solve it?

#10 Logan Likes Mary Anne!

Quiet, shy Mary Anne has been growing up lately . . . and the Baby-sitters aren't the only ones who've noticed. Logan Bruno likes Mary Anne! He has a dreamy southern accent, he's awfully cute — and he wants to join the Baby-sitters Club. Life in the club has never been this complicated — or this fun!

#11 Kristy and the Snobs

The kids in Kristy's new neighborhood aren't very friendly. In fact they're . . . well, snobs. They laugh at everything — even Kristy's poor old collie, Louie. Kristy's fighting mad. But if anyone can beat a Snob attack, it's the Baby-sitters club. And that's just what they're going to do!

#12 Claudia and the New Girl

Claudia really likes Ashley, the new girl at school. Ashley's the only one who takes Claudia seriously. Soon, Claudia's spending so much time with Ashley that she doesn't have time for baby-sitting — or her old friends. And they don't like it one bit!

148

#13 Good-bye Stacey, Good-bye

There are lots of tears when the Baby-sitters hear the news: Stacey and her family are moving back to New York. The club members can't think of a special enough way to send Stacey off. They want to give her much more than a party. But how do you say good-bye to your best friend?

#14 Hello, Mallory

Mallory Pike has always been good at baby-sitting her younger brothers and sisters. But is she good enough to join the Baby-sitters Club? The club members go overboard giving Mallory baby-sitting tests. Mallory's getting pretty fed up. . . . Maybe she'll just start a baby-sitting business of her own!

#15 Little Miss Stoneybrook . . . and Dawn

Mrs. Pike wants Dawn to help prepare Margo and Claire for the Little Miss Stoneybrook contest. And Dawn wants her charges to win! The only trouble is . . . Karen, Myriah, and Charlotte enter the contest, too. And nobody's sure where the competition is fiercer: at the pageant — or at the Baby-sitters Club!

#16 Jessi's Secret Language

Jessi had a hard time fitting in to Stoneybrook. But things got a lot better once she became a member of the Baby-sitters Club! Now Jessi has her biggest challenge yet — baby-sitting for a deaf boy. And in order to communicate with him, Jessi must learn his secret language.

#17 Mary Anne's Bad-Luck Mystery

Mary Anne finds a note in her mailbox. *"Wear this bad-luck charm,"* it says, *"OR ELSE."* Mary Anne's got to do what the note says. But who sent the charm? And why did they send it to Mary Anne? If the Baby-sitters don't solve this mystery soon, their bad luck might never stop!

#18 Stacey's Mistake

Stacey's so excited! She's invited her friends from the Baby-sitters Club down to New York City for a long weekend. But what a mistake! The Baby-sitters are *way* out of place in the big city. Does this mean Stacey can't be the Baby-sitters' friend anymore?

#19 Claudia and the Bad Joke

Claudia's not worried when she hears she has to baby-sit for Betsy, a great practical joker. How much trouble could a little girl cause? *Plenty* . . . and now Claudia might even quit the club. It's time for the Baby-sitters to teach Betsy a lesson. The joke war is on!

#21 Mallory and the Trouble With Twins

Mallory thinks baby-sitting for the Arnold twins will be easy money. They're so adorable! Marilyn and Carolyn may be cute . . . but they're also spoiled brats. It's a baby-sitting nightmare — and Mallory's not giving up!

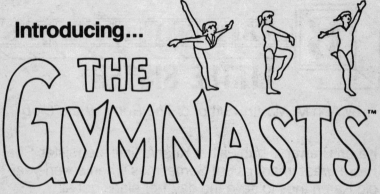